And we know that all things work together for good to those who love God, to those who are the called according to His purpose

-Romans 8:28

Foreword

The outlaw gangs of the Old West were romanticized in dime novels and the press until many, like Jesse James and Butch Cassidy, became folk heroes instead of the vicious killers they were. The truth is, these blood-thirsty, greedy men's quest for money and notoriety terrorized towns and the countryside. They left hundreds of innocent people murdered in their rampages.

Shootouts mesmerized the public, though only a few were due to feuds like the Gunfight at the O.K. Corral. Most pitted the gang against lawmen, who were the true heroes of the Old West.

Hearts haven't changed. The gangs of today—from Chicago Street gangs to Mexican cartels to ISIS—are even more dangerous. Evil people are still drawn to gangs, and we shouldn't be surprised. This is the devil's world. But we can rejoice because Jesus has overcome the world!

Chapter 1

Wyoming, 1879

Urgent rapping shook the front door, shattering the quiet in Jeannie Baylor's parlor. Her crochet hook flew from her hand to summersault in the air and ping across her freshly scrubbed wooden floor.

Nerves at full attention, Jeannie exchanged a startled glance with Pauline Weeks, her neighbor and houseguest. They both shot to their feet.

"Who in the world?" Pauline dropped her knitting in the basket by her chair.

Jeannie had no notion who it might be. Her and Pa's ranch was situated as far from civilization as any in the region. People didn't come visiting unannounced, especially after full dark. Near bedtime.

Anxiety glued her to the floor for the space of a breath, then she marched forward with forced confidence. She was about to grab Pa's Winchester hanging by the door when a familiar male voice came from outside. "It's me, Willie."

Relief began to swoosh out of her until she remembered even a friend coming this time of night spelled trouble.

She unlatched the door and Willie crossed the threshold. He was her dear friend, Rose's, tall, lanky husband, and enough worry etched his weathered features to make Jeannie's pulse kick up.

Willie didn't bother with greetings. "Rose fell down the back steps."

"Mercy sakes." Pauline pressed a hand to her heart and swayed like she might topple over. Rose was her daughter.

Willie swished his hand in the air, palm out.

"She's fine, Ma. I went for the doctor, and he said she and the baby would be all right, but she has to stay in bed until the baby comes."

Poor Rose. She must be terrified for her little one. Jeannie counted on her fingers. The baby wasn't due for another month.

"I'm sorry, Jeannie. I know Ma was supposed to stay with you while your pa's on the cattle drive, but I can't manage without her. Can't leave Rose alone while I do the chores, and there's Billy." Billy was Willie's five-year-old son from a former marriage and a handful for even a strong, healthy woman.

"I'll go get my things," Pauline said.

Worry for Rose crowded Jeannie's mind while Willie stared at his boots. He slapped his thigh, startling her. "Why don't you pack up and come with us, Jeannie. Your pa wouldn't want you staying way out here by yourself."

He was right about that. Pa had asked Pauline to stay with Jeannie to help run the ranch in his absence. Pauline's late husband and Pa had traveled west together over twenty years ago. They'd settled here in the foothills of the Tetons because the forests yielded the lumber for the houses and outbuildings, the mountains provided fresh water streams, and the valleys yielded abundant grass, though their cattle had to wander wide for grazing.

Jeannie thought it the most beautiful land on earth. Trouble was, it were so isolated, with no neighbors to call on when trouble came. The Baylors and Jameses had nobody to depend on but themselves. She'd love to go to Rose, who was more like a sister than a friend, but how could she?

Chores had to be done here too. Hard work had strengthened her over the years, but she had to admit it took her twice as long to do most ranch jobs as a man. And there was still the housework. Without Pauline's help, she didn't know how she'd get it all done.

Her silence prompted Willie. "Go with us now.

I can come over here once a day and take care of the stock. The rest can wait until Mr. Baylor gets back."

Willie James wasn't thinking straight. They lived seven miles apart. It would take hours just to come and go, not to mention the time it would take to care for the stock. She couldn't let him do that.

She plopped her fists on her waist. "You will not, and I will not. I can do anything that has to be done around here, and if I can't, it'll wait as you say. Just make sure you take care of my very best friend in all the world, Willie James, or you'll answer to me."

"You know I'll do that."

"Then it's settled. It's not the first time I've had the place to myself, and I've managed. But you can't leave Rose for anything. Who knows when you'll have to go back for the doctor?"

Pauline came back into the room, carrying her carpetbag. "I'm sure Jeannie will be all right for a few days, Willie." Her gaze traveled the room as if looking for something she might have missed before settling on Jeannie. "We better get going, dearie. Rose shouldn't be left alone too long."

Willie took Pauline's bag. "I asked Doc to stay with her till we got back." He started to turn, then swiveled a glance back to Jeannie. "I almost clean forgot. Rose asks if you have that cloak you were crocheting for her. The bedroom's not heated, and she has to drape a blanket over her shoulders when sitting propped up. The cloak will be more comfortable, she's thinking."

"I'm not quite finished with the cloak, but I can have it ready to bring with me when I come visiting Sunday." The Baylors and Jameses, along with Pauline, met every Sunday for dinner, visiting, and Bible study. Since the nearest church was far away in Rock Bend, they'd formed their own little church.

Pauline grabbed Jeannie in a hug that squeezed the breath out of her. "You take care of yourself and don't work too hard—but I know you will."

"Thank you for all your help." Jeannie kissed the older woman's wrinkled brow. "You just take care of Rose. Tell her I'll be thinking of and praying for her."

"And we'll be praying for you, dearie." Pauline patted Jeannie's shoulder. "Let's go, Willie. It'll be after mid-night before we get home."

They were at the door when another thought snagged Jeannie's muddled brain. "Oh, wait." She marched to the small bookshelf that held all her books. After stacking the treasured tomes in her arms, she scurried toward Willie. "Here, take these. I won't have time to read, and they'll help Rose pass the time."

Willie balanced the stack in the crook of his free arm and stepped aside for Pauline to clear the doorway.

Jeannie waited with her ear pressed to the door until the creaking of her neighbors' buckboard faded. No silence was quite as profound as a house bereft of human companionship, and for all her boasting that she could manage, an unsettled feeling stalked her back to her chair.

Well, she'd have to get used to it. Pa wouldn't be back for another week, if then.

When all traces of winter was gone and spring calving over, Pa had joined in with other ranchers in western Wyoming to round up the steers and drive them to the Medicine Bow stockyard.

She was used to solitude. Even Rose and her family lived too far except for a Sunday visit. But sometimes Jeannie wished they all lived closer to town. Close enough to go to church and maybe even meet a beau. Rose's marriage last year had Jeannie thinking about her lack of prospects.

When she and Rose turned seventeen, they'd begun praying earnestly for God to send them a husband—if that was His will, of course. Then Rose's pa died suddenly and Pauline decided to sell the ranch. Willie James came with his young son and a proposition. He didn't have enough money to buy the ranch, but he'd work for Pauline until he had enough money saved for the purchase.

The inevitable happened when Rose and Willie fell in love. Willie and Billy moved in as a part of the family. God had answered Rose's prayer.

But that didn't mean it was God's plan for Jeannie. Barring some miracle, she saw no hope for a husband or a future beyond Pa's small ranch. Maybe God expected her to stay here and take care of Pa during his declining years. Then she'd have to sell the ranch. And by that time, she'd be an old maid.

That was all right. If God wanted her to be married, He'd bring the right man into her life, like He had for Rose.

Enough stewing over her problems. She had to get back to work on that cloak. Anything she could do to make Rose more comfortable while she lay in bed worrying about her unborn child, Jeannie would do. But where could she snatch the extra time to complete the cloak before Sunday?

She hadn't even reached the place to make the slits for the arm holes. That would be tricky since Rose wanted pockets worked inside so she'd have a place to tuck a handkerchief or coins. Trouble was each row of the lower part of the cloak had so many stitches, it took several minutes to get from one end to the other.

After retrieving her crochet hook, she set the tool flashing in and out of the wool so fast concern for Rose and her own loneliness drifted to the back of her mind.

She was at the point of turning a new row, when something bumped against the house, jarring the window of the house. The hook again flew from her hand and clinked across the floor as she felt the fine hair rise on her neck. Likely as not, the wind had blown a limb off one of the pines. It had happened before.

Holding her breath, she let other possibilities

march through her brain. It might be an animal. A large animal. Elk roamed out of the forests at times. As did bears. Grizzlies.

Elk posed no danger to anything other than her vegetable garden, but bears would go after the livestock. They'd already taken a calf this year. And bears sometimes tried to break into houses. With success.

Several moments of quiet ticked off before her reason took over. The Lord didn't give her a spirit of fear, and she was a capable ranch woman. If Papa were home. If she were not alone, she wouldn't be scared out of her wits.

Papa wasn't here, but the Spirit of the Lord reigned over this house. Nothing to fear. Still, she had to know.

Crossing the room in jerky steps to the parlor's lone window, she pulled the curtains back, and peered into the semi-darkness. A near full moon hung in the clear sky illuminating the trees.

A shiver darted up her back. No wind stirred.

Not one pine needle, or leaf of shrub, nor one blade of grass, moved. The night was as still as she'd ever known it to be. Swallowing pure fear, she moved the curtains further and strained to look to the right and left. Nothing stirred. All she heard was her own fitful breathing.

If a bear lurked, the cows would be bawling. The chickens squawking. She drew in a lungful of air and let it out slowly before dropping the curtains and returning to her seat.

Just her silly imagination brought on by Willie's surprise visit and Pauline's leaving.

She searched the floor for her crochet hook. A flash of metal revealed its hiding place, under the edge of the sofa. She retrieved it and unrolled a generous portion of the soft tan wool, guessing it to be enough to finish the row.

Her heartbeat slowed as she got back to work on the cloak. Normally, a bump in the night wouldn't have bothered her at all, but she'd feel a lot better when morning came.

Chores, hers and Pa's, would keep her occupied during the daylight hours. She was used to hard work. Ever since Mama died when Jeannie was fourteen, she'd had a heavy workload. If she could just make it through the night.

Nights were the hardest, and though the days were growing longer, without Pauline's help, the household chores would last past nightfall.

She settled into her well-worn nook and tried to concentrate. Working in the arm holes required focus. Stitches had to be counted on each side for uniformity. Soon her hook was pushing in, grabbing yarn, and pulling through at a steady rate.

Concentration shattered when another loud bump crashed into the side of the house. Her heart reared against her rib cage like a wild stallion trying to escape. She clutched her throat in an attempt to control the terror threatening to choke her.

Something was going on out there, and Pa

wasn't here to investigate. Which meant she had to. She raced to the window. The second bump seemed to come further back of the house, near the kitchen. If it was a bear trying to find a way in, it would be drawn to the kitchen. She looked out the other side, slanting her gaze in that direction.

Again, nothing appeared out of the ordinary. The chicken coop was back there. If a wild animal got after them, they'd be in a frenzy.

Not a peep disturbed the calm.

What if one of their stock got loose? She squinted to make out the lines of the barn. Pat and Ned, the two workhorses, shared the space with Dolly, their prize Guernsey cow. Losing any one of them was unthinkable. The far coral held several heifers waiting for the bull Pa would be bringing back with him.

Had she made sure to secure the horses and cow in their stalls when she'd fed them earlier? She ought to check on them.

Pa's rifle waited for her in its wall rack beside

the door. He'd cleaned and oiled it before he left. She'd seen him load it. In a forced gait she crossed the floor and reached for the weapon.

She knew how to use the rifle. It was heavy, but she was a ranch woman with plenty of muscles—not as large as a man's, but hard as her callused hands. Lifting the gun as quietly and delicately as she might lift a tea pitcher at afternoon tea, she gripped it with one hand and raised the door's latch.

The squeal of hinges sent a cringe through her. With all the resolve she could muster, she widened the opening, sticking the rifle barrel in front of her, chest high. A step on the small covered front porch brought another squeak of loose floor board.

"Meow."

Jeannie jumped and gripped the rifle tighter, then almost laughed at her silly fear. It was Old Tom, the big gray tabby, too wild to pet, but not too wild to ask for handouts. She'd been trying to tame the cat. Relaxing her hold on the gun, she bent to touch Old Tom.

Before she could react, the rifle was jerked from her hands. From the side, long claw-like fingers closed like a vise around her flaying arm. In front of her a large whiskered face with demon eyes leered. Whether pulled by the claws or pushed by the demon, she was forced back into the house.

For a split second terror strangled Jeannie. Then she screamed.

Chapter 2

A woman's scream jolted Zak Collins from around the side of the house. All he caught was a flash of blue calico and curly brown hair before Clive and Horace obliterated the woman from view.

Clive swung a slit gaze toward Zak. "Get on in here, boy."

The command snapped with the force of a whip. As a boy, Zak had felt the sting of Clive's whip often enough that he now recoiled from the memory. He shoved his own motives for joining the gang aside and bolted up the cabin's steps. They'd brought an innocent woman into the fray. That changed everything. He slipped his Colt from the holster as he entered the room. They didn't know for sure who was inside. He'd watched the woman earlier as she took care of the stock. If there was a man about, wouldn't he be doing those chores? Unless he was plain sorry or injured. Lying in wait.

Now that he saw her up close, he realized she was younger than he'd thought. She was shy of twenty, for sure. A girl really.

Horace's shaggy red head popped out of another room. "No one in there." He still held the girl's rifle.

"Put your weapons away, boys." Clive still held a grip on the girl's forearm. "I'm sure this little gal's going to be friendly." As if to give her a chance to prove herself, he released her.

She crouched in a corner, her large, brown eyes giving them a terrified, mute appeal.

If Zak could give her any reassurance, he would. She looked so pathetic. But truth was, she had reason to be terrified. Both Clive and Horace were killers. Clive had killed one woman—no, make that two. He'd killed Zak's mother, as surely as if he'd broken her neck with his hands.

"You the only one here, gal?" Clive's question indicated he worried that man they'd watched leave the house earlier might come back.

The room gave evidence there was a man connected to this house. A pair of suspenders hung from a hook beside a bowler such as a man would wear to Sunday meeting. Work-worn boots, much too big for the woman, stood in the corner.

"What's the matter, gal. That cat got your tongue?" Both Clive and Horace guffawed.

"My name is Jeannie." Her voice burst through surprisingly strong for one cowering in fear for her life. Her chin tilted upward as she leveled a contemptuous stare at Clive.

Zak's muscles tightened, ready to protect Jeannie from Clive's wrath, knowing no one challenged Clive without repercussion.

"Well, Jeannie, answer my question."

Jeannie wasn't backing down either. "What are you doing here? What do you want?"

Clive laughed again, looking back over his shoulder at Horace and then Zak. "What do you think, boys? That's a right fair question. After all, we weren't invited." He shifted a look of pure evil at Jeannie. "The boys know I'm not usually fair, but I'm going to answer you this one time." Abruptly, his voice blared like a holiness preacher trying to wake the flock. "We're outlaws, gal. Who'd you think we were? The church welcoming committee?"

"I *am* a preacher, Clive." Horace spurted a chortle that dribbled spit in his nasty red beard. Zak turned his gaze from the nauseating sight. Horace had pretended to be a preacher while he robbed that little country church of all their funds.

Clive ignored both of them, keeping his gaze on Jeannie. "We have a posse, a big one from Cheyenne looking for us, and we need a hideout."

The old man grimaced, and Zak waited to see

if Clive's reoccurring stomach pain would lay him out. Clive had a tumor growing in his stomach and would die before much longer. Whether the tumor got him before the gallows did was anyone's guess. He kept a supply of opium to eat for the pain, but his supply was growing short.

Clive twisted his lips in a gesture of bravado. "This is gonna be our hideout, Jeannie. Now, when's your man coming back?"

"I don't have a man. My pa's on a cattle drive."

"What about the fellow we saw here earlier?"

"He's...a neighbor...coming for his mother-in-law."

"Well, let's hope neither he nor your pa get back before we leave, or we'll have to get rid of them."

Jeannie gasped and the knuckles of her clenched hands turned white.

Clive's haggard features bunched again. He made his way to the kitchen table in the back of the room and fell into one of the chairs. "We hadn't had anything to eat since daybreak. Rustle us up some grub and be fast about it. You got something ready?"

Jeannie's glance latched onto Zak's for the first time. Her tear glazed eyes tugged at his heart, and everything in him wanted to go to her aid. He couldn't. Not yet.

Something more than sympathy moved him. She was a beautiful woman, in a wholesome, unadorned way. Her hair, parted in the middle, framed a lovely Madonna-like face.

Long, dark lashes fluttered and rested for a moment on her pale cheeks before she spoke. "I have a pot of chicken stew and biscuits I'd been planning to eat on for a couple of days."

"Then get it on the table," Clive barked.

"I'll have to warm it a bit." Jeannie finally released the wall she was hugging. She wound her way around the table and to the iron stove. After poking life in the fire, she stirred the stew and added water to the coffee pot from the water reservoir.

Clive and Horace watched her like vultures, but for different reasons. Horace's eyes bugged as a depraved sailor's might when setting his sights on a woman after a long voyage. Clive's eyes were menacing, revealing little soul, like a man who cared little for his own life, much less others.

With a loud grunt, Horace pushed his bulk onto the only other chair at the table. A third ladder-back chair stood in the corner near the stove. Zak would leave that one for Jeannie. He dragged up a step stool from the near wall and straddled it.

Propping his elbows on the plank tabletop, he studied Jeannie as she worked in jerky movements. Grinding coffee beans. Shoving a pan of biscuits in the oven. Stirring the contents of the stew pot. She flitted from one task to the other like a butterfly in a petunia patch.

Mostly, she kept her back to the men, and Zak couldn't blame her. They must be a gristly sight.

She, on the other hand, was about as pretty as any woman had a right to be. Her shining brown hair cascaded in curls down her back, tied with a blue ribbon. She filled out her faded blue calico dress beautifully as the skirt swayed with her movement.

He was so mesmerized by the lovely lady, she surprised him by setting the first bowl in front of him. He straightened and, drawing the dish closer, stared straight into her soft, brown eyes fringed by sweeping long lashes. "Thank you, ma'am."

She tried to appear calm, and might have gotten away with it, except for the vein in her neck, throbbing crazily. "You're welcome."

"Just because we're ugly don't mean we ain't hungry," Clive growled.

Like a shot, she turned to dish up two more bowls, then plopped three spoons in the middle of the table.

Zak followed her moves as she took the biscuits out of the oven, holding the hot pan with the corner of her apron. When she set them down, her gaze again traveled to Zak. He read fear and pleading in her eyes.

He wished he could help her. Why did Clive have to stop here? Terrorize a helpless woman? Only a ruthless killer like Clive would threaten a woman. But he'd abused and finally killed his own wife.

Since then, Clive's depravity grew, and he had a talent for ferreting out the weak and defenseless. Before they'd pulled that stage robbery, they stopped at a farmhouse for a meal. Not knowing who they were, the old couple had treated them with kindness and invited them to their table.

If Zak had any notion of what Clive had in mind, he'd have stopped him, even though that would have jeopardized their plans. They'd given their hosts a pleasant good-bye on the porch. Then after they'd saddled up and were no further than a few yards, Clive had shouted, "Wait."

Naturally, the old man and woman stopped in their tracks to look back, as did Zak and Horace.

With no warning at all, Clive had raised his rifle and shot, first the old man, then the old woman. They'd fallen into each other's arms.

Zak had jumped from his mount and ran to the couple.

"Stop boy!"

But Zak hadn't stopped until he confirmed the couple was truly dead. "Why'd you do that, Clive? They didn't know who we were."

"Boy, you don't know nothing. After we hit that stage, the law's going to be crawling all over. That old couple could've described us. We can't leave witnesses. It's us or them, remember that."

Zak remembered well as he looked into Jeannie's eyes. He'd find some way to save her— even if he had to kill Clive to do it.

The nugget of a plan started forming in his brain.

After long moments, she backed up and started for the front parlor. Clive's arm shot out, stopping her in mid-stride. "Whoa, gal. Sit over there in the corner. We have to keep an eye on you."

"When are you going to leave?"

"Well now, we don't know." The menacing tone stayed in Clive's voice. "Zak's going to check out that little town in a couple of days and see if the posse's moved on. In the meantime, let's try to get along."

Her shoulders slumped as she made her way to the chair by the stove.

Silence stretched long and oppressive. Then the quiet broke with clinking spoons on china and Horace's slurping like a hog digging into his slop.

Jeannie was a good cook. She'd make someone a good wife—if she lived.

Clive sat looking ahead, chewing a biscuit like a cow working on her cud. He couldn't eat much at the time because the tumor took up most of his stomach room. His weight had fallen off like a dog's in a deserted mining camp. The angular bones of his face gave him a grotesque appearance in the lamplight. He wouldn't live much longer. Unfortunately, he still had enough time to add several more notches on his gun.

Normally Zak had a good appetite, and the stew was delicious, but after one bowl, he couldn't eat another bite. On the other hand, Horace demanded Jeannie refill his bowl twice.

Clive threw down his spoon with a jarring crash. His chair scraped the floor as he got up. "Come on with me, boy. Horace, you keep an eye on that girl."

Zak held back. He didn't like leaving Jeannie alone with Horace. He'd seen the fat man's leering glance travel from her hair to the hem of her dress, lingering too long over her curves. He had an idea of how to save Jeannie. It was a preposterous plan. Unlikely to work. A long shot. But like a poker player caught with a losing hand, he had to try.

Chapter 3

Out on the porch, the old outlaw scratched a Lucifer against the weathered plank. It burst into flame, lighting the stubby cheroot Clive puffed.

The familiar, nasty smell blew straight into Zak's face.

Clive pointed with the cigar. "You need to get the horses bedded down—just leave them saddled. Don't know what we might have to get out fast." He didn't look back but stomped toward his horse and took the rope hanging from the saddle.

Zak untied his and Horace's horses. "What do you need with the rope?"

Clive pulled the cheroot from his slobbering mouth and gave him that are-you-stupid look.

"Whadda think? To tie up that gal—Jeannie. We need to keep her for the duration. She's a good cook. Anyways, we're all tired and can't keep a watch on her, though I guess you'd like to." His laugh turned into a cough.

For the duration.

The horses could wait. If Zak knew anything about Clive Stubbs—and he did—the old man wouldn't deal unless there was something in the pot for him. "You're right about that. She is a looker. What do you think about letting her join the gang?"

Clive almost swallowed his cigar. "Join the gang? She wouldn't join the gang, even though she was giving you moony eyes. Nah, we don't need a woman, even if she would agree."

"She might—if I marry her."

Clive went into another coughing jag, and Zak added, "I bet I could sweet talk her into it before the night's over." If he could get her alone long enough to explain his plan.

"I know you're joshing." Clive threw the cigar down and ground it into the dirt. "Miss Respectable, Jeannie, won't marry you, boy. Yeah, she likes your looks, but that don't mean she'd marry you. You're an outlaw. No decent woman will ever marry you. Remember, I told you that when you joined up. The only women you can get are saloon gals and strumpets." He started to walk off.

"No, hear me out, Clive. Horace is a preacher. He could marry us and—"

"Horace used to be a preacher. He was defrocked by that church he cleaned out."

"But he thinks he's still a preacher, and Jeannie won't know the difference."

Clive squinted until the sagging skin around his eye sockets all but hid his eyes. "Even if you could pull that off, we don't need a woman on the trail. She'd slow us down—plus, the boss won't like it."

Zak drew in a lungful of sweet, late spring air

tinged with the fragrance of wildflowers. He'd noticed Jeannie had set out potpourri balls throughout the house. How could such a lovely scent exist in a world with Clive's stench?

"She could make herself useful on the trail cooking. The Jackal won't even talk to me unless I prove myself. You said it yourself. Don't know a better way to prove myself than by killing my wife with him a witness."

That hit Clive square between the eyes. It was the only time Zak could recall being able to flummox the old cuss. He actually bent forward, peering up at Zak through his shaggy brows like he thought someone else had taken over Zak's body. "Are you telling me you're going to pretend marry that little gal in there? Partake of her...charms...for the better part of the two weeks it'll take us to get to the Jackal's hideout? Then put a bullet through her pretty head?"

"You told me it's one of the Jackal's rules that a man has to kill someone who's a threat to the gang. Jeannie's a threat."

"She's a threat now for sure, but there's no need to marry her. Just kill her tonight."

Zak nudged his hat back, giving himself a moment to control his tone. Clive could read a man's manners better than most. "Maybe I want to partake of her charms a while. And remember, I'm not on a wanted poster. Likely as not, the Jackal wouldn't believe I killed her, even if you and Horace said so."

Clive twisted his thin lips. "You're right about that. The Jackal don't trust anyone." His faded eyes narrowed. "All the same, I believe you're bluffing." He stretched his brows and dipped his head to stare through Zak. "But I agree—killing your wife in front of the Jackal ort to show you're depraved enough to satisfy him. Just remember one thing. If you don't kill her, the Jackal will kill both of you."

Zak forced a smile. "I'm aware of the consequences."

Clive laughed and slapped him on the

shoulder. "You've come a long way, boy. I know you don't have a stomach for killing. That's why I haven't expected you to—up till now."

Tension seeped out of Zak. Clive had begrudgingly taken him on. Truth was, the old man didn't trust him. By insinuating he'd play the Jackal's evil game and kill Jeannie, he'd gained Clive's begrudging respect. But he wasn't fool enough to think the old man wouldn't strike like a rattler if he turned his back on him.

Zak had taken a calculated risk and won. If only he could dupe Clive long enough to effect Jeannie's escape.

Clive's features took on a rare thoughtful look. "Just don't let that woman go to your head, boy. A woman can do that, you know. You let them into your head and afore you know it, they have you eating out of their hands." Clive spat and Zak could swear it had blood in it.

The old man looked off to the tree line. "Truth is, I've have plans for you, boy. Wasn't going to tell you until we got to the boss's headquarters, but I might not make it."

Fear crawled up Zak's spine. Clive's plans were never good for anyone but him. Best to play along, though. Keep Clive in a good mood. Zak chuckled. "What kind of plans?"

"I been studying on it. I owe something to your ma." That was an understatement coming from the man who'd killed her. "Your ma was a good woman. A beautiful woman." He swiveled his gaze to Zak. "Been thinking a lot about your ma lately. She'd want you to have a good life. This is what I'm going to do. After we get our loot, I'm going to give you most of it."

Zak froze. Did he hear that right? Clive had cared for nothing but money ever since Zak knew him. He'd spent his life taking money by fair means or foul—mostly foul. "You're joshing."

"No, I owe it to your ma. All I'm going to need is enough to keep my opium in supply, and I won't be needing that long. Think I'll make my way to

San Francisco. They have a good quality of opium there. Maybe I'll get me a good supply of women, too, for as long as I last. Even with the women, I shouldn't need but a quarter of the loot."

"I don't know what to say." There was plenty to say, but he'd best keep it to himself.

"Nothing to say. You'll take your share and three-fourths of mine. You can go on to Arizona territory. Maybe even get yourself a respectable wife. Settle down. No one will ever know you rode with the most notorious gang in the west."

Zak supposed every man staring death in the face might try to right past wrongs, but there was nothing Clive could say or do to change Zak's opinion of him. The old man was as low-down as the dirt on his boot sole and not to be trusted. "I appreciate that. I know I haven't been doing my part, but I promise I'll keep my eyes peeled on Jeannie. You won't have to concern yourself with her."

Clive's smile was as stiff as a starched shirt

collar. "I don't doubt you'll keep her close to the chest. Just don't let her trick you. I've let my guard down with a woman too often, even your ma." He shook his balding gray head. "But she was a good woman. I ort to call her an angel." He stretched his turkey neck to stare into the star-spangled sky. "Guess she's an angel proper now. Who knows? Maybe I'll wind up with her up there. Wouldn't that surprise us all?"

Zak had to look away. If there was a just God, Clive would wind up as far from heaven as anyone could. "Well, I'll take care of the horses, then come in to talk to Jeannie."

"Don't think you ort to do that. I got me a notion about how to convince Miss Look-Down-Her-Nose she has no other choice but to marry you tonight."

Zak was untying his horse's reins. He dropped them and whirled around. "Tonight! I need a day or two to get her warm to the idea."

"You ort to be able to warm a woman up faster

than that. Get the horses settled. She'll be ready for you by then." The nasty tone was back in Clive's voice. He stalked off to the house.

Zak started to run after him. No telling what Clive was up to. But what could Zak do?

All the tension was back and settled like a wad of undigested fear in his stomach. He jerked the reins of all three long-legged buckskins and made for the barn in wide strides.

Chapter 4

Jeannie hugged herself, glancing occasionally at the disgusting man slurping his third bowl of chicken stew. She wished those other two would come back. Actually, she wished only the young one came back. Something about him let her know he was on her side. At any rate, she didn't want to be alone with the hulking red-headed man left to guard her.

Mostly she prayed, but being too terrified to think coherently, she couldn't get past *help me, Lord*. Would He? If she had enough faith? No, God didn't work that way. He didn't always come to the rescue, even if you were in desperate need. Even if you wrung your heart out. She'd realized that when Ma died. She'd skinned her knees praying, but Ma died anyway.

Why did God answer some prayers and not others? Did he favor some over others? No, He didn't even spare His Son, Jesus. Jesus had prayed the night before His crucifixion. But He'd ended with "Not My will, but Yours be done."

She couldn't expect to be treated any better. In the end, you always had to accept God's will.

It would be helpful, if, when she closed her eyes and opened them, she'd find all this a nightmare. It didn't work, though. The big galoot was still there, and she presumed the other two lurked outside.

If only the outlaw would choke, but what good would that do? His smelly cohorts would remain.

Why did this have to happen with Pa gone? But in a way, it was better he not be here. Pa would have fought, and they would've killed him. *They might kill you,* the little demon of fear whispered.

She closed her eyes again, strangling a napkin in her hands.

A loud belch brought her to attention. Horace had his elbows propped on the table, staring at her like she was dessert. "Mighty fine dinner, Jeannie. Come on over here and let me thank you."

She swallowed the knot of fear lodged in her throat. "No thanks is necessary."

The chair scraped as he twisted around. "I say it is. Come on and get in my lap." He patted his knee.

Her chin shot up. "I could never be that familiar with a...any man."

Horace chuckled. "I'm thinking we're gonna get mighty familiar, Jeannie. You got a feller?"

Should she say yes? If he thought she had someone who cared enough about her to come after anyone who hurt her, he might leave her alone. It was a weak hope, and required lying. Was it ever right to lie, even to save your life? Surely God would understand.

"No."

"You're probably too young. Bet you're not over sixteen."

"I'm eighteen."

"A woman grown." Horace laughed. "Then it's time you got familiar with a man." He skewered her with the look of a bull to a penned cow, and slapped his thick thigh. "I expect you're tired. Get on my lap, honey, and I'll rock you to sleep."

He was toying with her and enjoying it like a cat enjoys playing with a mouse. Her heart hammered so loud, she heard the pounding in her ears. She grabbed each side of the chair and, at the same time, wrapped her feet around the chair legs. If he came for her, he'd have to take the chair with her.

The front door slammed and one pair of boots jarred the floor. Jeannie let out the breath she'd been holding and fixed her gaze on the kitchen opening. *Please God, let it be Zak.*

Clive's ugly face rounded the corner, crashing

her hopes.

Horace twisted his rusty colored moustache. "I'd be glad to keep watch on Jeannie tonight. Does Zak still have that old pair of cuffs? I could cuff her to me when we go to bed."

"No need for that. Have you ever performed a wedding ceremony? You know the words?"

Horace reared back, cocking one bushy brow. "Shore, I've hitched over a dozen couples when I was with the church. What you up to?"

"We're going to have a wedding."

Jeannie glanced from Clive to Horace. These men weren't just dangerous. They were crazy.

Horace slid his gaze to Jeannie. She shook her head so hard, the ribbon loosened her hair. "Not me. No. Never."

Clive didn't even spare her a look. "Horace, you're going to hitch Zak to Jeannie. He'll be able to keep an eye on her as her husband."

Jeannie shot from her chair. "I'm not marrying anyone. Nothing you do can make me."

Clive swiveled around so fast she jumped back.

"Is that so? I'm thinking you'll change your mind when you know the alternative." Malice darted from his cold eyes. "If it was up to Horace and me, we wouldn't need marriage to get what we wanted, but my boy still carries around his ma's religious teachings."

"Too bad his religious teachings don't keep him from stealing and running with a gang."

"Stealing's different," Horace said. "We're kind of like Robin Hood, stealing from the rich to give to the poor. And we're the poor." He chortled at his joke.

"Shut up." Clive slammed his fist down on the table, rattling the dishes. "As I was saying, the boy's taken a liking to you, and he wants to take you with us."

The cords in her neck tightened, threatening to cut off her windpipe. She had to cough to draw in enough air to speak. "Well, I don't like him. I won't marry him, and I certainly won't go with you." Her voice spoke confidence, but there was no force behind her words and he knew it.

"I know how women are, Miss High-and-Mighty. A woman may hate her husband at first, but she falls in line soon enough. That's the way it was with both my wives, and you're no different. A couple days of Zak's sweet talking, and you'll do anything he says."

"I'd rather die."

"All right. That can be arranged, too. But what about your pa? We could wait here until he returns and lay him out before he gets through the door."

Panic froze the retort in Jeannie's throat. This mad man would do just that. She had to think of a way of escape before Pa got back. Maybe Zak would be reasonable. She'd noticed a bit of sanity in his eyes—a bit of humanity too. Surely he wouldn't force a woman to marry him. She willed the fear to the recesses of her mind.

The sound of the front door had them all looking that way. Clive drew his gun, and when

Zak came into view, holstered it. "Come on in, boy. Your bride is ready."

Zak walked toward Jeannie, and she backed up. But not before getting a whiff of Pa's soap. It was just common lye soap, but she'd gathered woodland berries and herbs, and seeped them in the soap. The scent was pungent and cut through the stench clinging to Pa after he mucked the horses' stalls. In spite of the situation facing her, Jeannie found the smell comforting. Zak had taken the time to wash up. For her? A man with that kind of concern would surely stand up to his pa.

"Take her hand, Zak," Clive snapped. "Horace, get on with it."

Jeannie jerked back as Zak reached for her hand and stared into his eyes that had taken on the menacing angry green of an approaching hailstorm. "Your father has convinced me you have some decency in you. Tell him this is a farce. This man," she inclined her head to Horace, "isn't qualified to marry anyone."

"Am too. I've been ordained."

"And serve the Lord by robbing and killing?"

"Don't matter. A minister of the gospel stays that way."

"Shut up," Clive shouted again. "I've got to get to bed, and Zak, you've got to take your bride to bed."

Zak reached around and clenched her hand, pulling it by force to make her stand beside him, facing Horace. Loosening his grip, he gave her hand a gentle squeeze as any groom would to give his bride confidence. Oddly enough, it did give her comfort. But it was short-lived.

She gave him a sidelong glance. He was just an actor in a play. When the curtains fell, he'd go back to being an outlaw, but her life would be changed forever. Her life might as well be over.

He knew this was all a pretense and was eagerly playing his part. Her first impression of Zak had been right. In any other situation, he'd be a nice man, but she pegged him for a coward, an outlaw who didn't have his heart in it, but too weak to stand up to his pa. Disappointment left a bitter taste in her mouth. Only God could save her.

She barely listened as Horace gave Zak his vows to repeat. Vows? What a farce.

Clive propped on the edge of the table, his arms folded over his middle as if in pain. Something was wrong with his stomach as well as his brain and heart. That hallow look in his eyes suggested death hovered over the man, and only meanness kept his body and soul together.

Horace's bellow jerked her back to the moment at hand. "I said, do you take this man, Zak Collins, to be your lawfully wed husband."

Jeannie moved her lips, but no words came.

Clive pushed himself off the table. "Let me put it this way. Do you want us gone when your pa shows up?" Deep grooves etched his mouth and eye sockets.

She felt Zak tighten his hold. "No reason to threaten her," he said. "Give her some time."

"I reckon she's had enough time. We're just doing this to humor you, boy." He set his wicked stare on Jeannie. "Time's up, gal. Do you want us to leave your pa in one piece?"

Nausea roiled in her stomach. "Yes, I do."

Horace slapped his hands together. "I now pronounce you man and wife. You may now kiss the bride. Or I could if you want."

"Don't you ever dare touch her, Horace." For the first time Zak put steel behind his words.

"You can do your kissing in private." Clive pushed past them and opened the first door. "Is this your room, gal? Pink ruffled curtains. I'm guessing it is." He slung open the opposite door. "This must be your pa's. I'll take that. Horace, you sleep out here and keep your gun cocked."

Horace skirted around them on his way to the parlor. Zak didn't make a move while keeping a stranglehold on Jeannie's hand.

Clive swung back to them. "What are you waiting for? I swear, you're the sourest looking newlyweds I've ever seen. I should've had a talk with you, boy. It's customary for you to carry her across the threshold."

Zak drew in an audible breath and finally released Jeannie's hand.

She darted her gaze from left to right like a bird seeking a place to land. Then she felt strong arms under her knees as Zak lifted her in his arms. Stunned, her head pressed against his shoulder, she heard the rapid beating of his heart. For all his outward calm, he was nervous too—maybe even as scared as she was.

The familiar furnishings of her bedroom came into view. The highboy chest of drawers, the rocking chair Pa made for Ma, the rag rug anchoring the bed with its iron frame, the table with her wash bowl. From the mirror hanging above the wash bowl, she caught a glimpse of herself held in Zak's arms, like a trophy—the spoils of a battle.

Something stirred in her. Primitive and wild.

The desire to survive. If he thought she'd submit to his wicked plan, he was mistaken. He'd soon know she was as dangerous as a cornered cougar. She might appear docile, but she had a lot of fight in her.

She noticed the figurine of an angel sitting atop the highboy. Pa had surprised her with that porcelain statuette for her tenth birthday for no other reason than he'd thought it beautiful. Over the years, it had given her comfort as she imagined her guardian angel watching over her.

Zak stopped within reach of the highboy and kicked the door closed. As sure and fast as a frog's tongue darts out to capture its prey, Jeannie's hand shot out to take the figurine. She hid it in the folds of her skirt.

In two long strides, Zak brought her to the bed. Putting all her force into her booted foot, she kicked backward like a mule and about as hard. Even with the fabric layers of her dress, petticoat, and his jeans, the force of her kick made him buckle and gulp a sharp intake of breath.

"I'm not going to hurt you, Jeannie," he said through clenched teeth.

Well, she *was* going to hurt him. As much as possible. At the same moment he set her on the side of the bed, she drew back her secret weapon. With finger-snap speed, she struck him full in the face.

The porcelain angel thudded to the floor.

She expected his anger, yet nothing but disbelief sparked from his eyes. Blood oozed from a slash just under his right eye with smaller cuts running down his cheek. She took advantage of his surprise to dash toward the door.

His arm caught her around the waist, and he pulled her back to the bed. She bounced heels over head to land on the other side. He came after her around the bed so hard he slammed into the wall, shaking the whole room. She scrambled across the mattress, but he grabbed a handful of skirt, stopping her escape.

Zak climbed across the bed to pin her in. If she could just get one hand free, she could scratch down the uninjured side of his face or stab him in the eye. But he captured both her arms and pushed her down across the bed, leaning into her until their noses almost touched.

They both panted, trying to catch their breath, staring into each other's eyes.

Jeannie twisted and thrashed as much as the tiny bit of space allowed her.

With her arms secured, Zak took hold of her shoulders, shaking her none to gently. "Listen to me. I've never forced myself on a woman before, and I'm not going to start now. You've got to listen."

Did he expect her to trust him? She didn't know much about men, but she knew enough not to trust a man who ran with an outlaw gang.

He had her pinned down. All she could do was jerk her head with enough vigor to keep the springs creaking.

Zak raised his voice only a tad, as if he was afraid of being overheard. "I won't harm you, but you're in grave danger. Those two curs out there are cold-bloodied killers. They're woman killers, Jeannie, and it's going to take all our wits together to keep you alive."

She stopped her thrashing and searched his eyes. The moss colored orbs softened with sincerity and pleading.

He was telling the truth. "Why would you help me?"

"I guess because my ma taught me to respect women and defend them against evil men. I failed her, but maybe I'm trying to make it up to her. I swear to you I'm going to do everything I can to help you escape, but you have to hear me out. We can't fight each other."

Blood still oozed from where she'd injured him, though it was trying to congeal. A drop fell on her chin. She drew a deep breath. "I'll hear you out, but first let me wash your wound."

Chapter 5

Zak awoke to the rooster's crow. Why was he lying here on the floor instead of the cold, hard ground? He squinted to make out his surrounding in the dusky light and flinched. A flash of pain brought back details of the previous night. The gash under his right eye hurt like the blazes. She'd fought like a wildcat, landing a couple of good punches before they'd reached their truce. He admired her for that.

He'd pulled his pallet here in front of the door to make sure no one came in unannounced. Turning on his left side, he gasped as pain shot through his knee where Jeannie had kicked him.

After settling back down, he stared at the sliver of light coming under the door. The house was silent except for the persistent rooster. Did that mean Horace was up? When Zak had finally drifted off to sleep last night, Horace had been snoring hard enough to set the rafters flapping.

It wasn't the snoring that kept Zak awake last night, but rather, concern for Jeannie. After she'd made this pallet for him, they'd lain down in their respective beds. Thoughts careened through his brain keeping sleep at bay. Sleep evidently evaded Jeannie as well. He'd given her enough to consider to keep her awake. He'd asked her to trust him, but why would she?

In the deep silence of night, soft sounds came from under her covers, like a woman's muffled sobbing.

If Horace was awake, Zak had better get up too. He turned to his right side and decided to wait a few minutes. The room lay in shadows, and all he could make out of his little wildcat was her form.

She hadn't removed anything but her boots before going to bed.

He'd kept his boots on, never knowing when he might have to run.

The three of them hadn't had the pleasure of taking off their boots during the past several days. They hadn't changed clothes, and all smelled worse than a pack of skunks. Maybe it wouldn't have mattered to him if they hadn't come up on Jeannie. Sometime today he'd find a way to take a bath. And yes, get those other two polecats to do the same.

They'd expect Jeannie to wash their clothes, but Zak refused to put more on her than possible. He'd ask her for some soap and do the washing himself. What else did he have to do, holed up as they were? Except protecting Jeannie from those killers.

Clive and Horace would waste time playing checkers or poker, unless they drank themselves stupid. That was the best Zak could hope for.

As the room lightened, Jeannie's features came into view. Who would have thought such a beautiful woman lived out here in the middle of the wilderness? Like coming up on an exquisite rose or an exotic orchid on the forest floor. Her silky brown hair splayed over the pillow, hair he'd like to stroke. Long dark lashes cut crescents on pale cheeks. Full lips, slighted parted, meant to be kissed.

Whoa. He'd better knock those thoughts clean out of his mind. But he couldn't help imagining what it would be like if he could court a woman like that. Win her heart. Too bad a man in his position couldn't hope to have a respectable woman.

Still, the sight of her twisted his gut, reminding him he'd have to fight his own instincts to keep her trust.

She stirred and opened her eyes, looking around the room as if wondering where she was.

He managed to stand. "Good morning,

Jeannie. Guess we'd better get started. I'll help you with your morning chores before you cook breakfast."

She stared at him for a long moment, then threw the covers off.

He cleared his throat. "I'll step out so you can change clothes. I suggest, hum..." He coughed, embarrassed as a schoolboy at what he had to say. "It'd be best for you to use the chamber pot. It might not be safe using the outhouse." He ran his fingers through his hair and rubbed his neck before opening the door.

"Thank you." Jeannie's voice was as soft as a turtledove's coo.

After scanning the parlor and finding no one about, Zak moved through the silent house and thumbed the back door latch. He slipped through the opening and pulled the door closed behind him.

An early morning fog shrouded the outbuildings and trees. Where had Horace gotten to? Clive would likely be sleeping off the effects of his opium until noon. One of these days, he might eat too much of the drug and never wake up. A lot of opium eaters did that. But they wouldn't be lucky enough for Clive to do himself in.

He walked around the periphery of the corral and barn. Rounding the corner of the far side, and a new stench hit him in the face. Squeals and grunts identified the source. Zak counted a sow and six half grown pigs. They all ran toward him as far as their pen would allow, obviously expecting him to bring the morning slop. He passed the pig pen, his eyes still peeled on the woods.

A rustling on the forest floor made him freeze. Maybe it was his imagination, but it sounded slow and deliberate—like a human.

Could it be the posse had caught up with them? Zak, along with Clive and Horace, had scouted out this area the previous day, and the next house was at least five miles away. No one would be casually walking around these woods.

With his heart hammering his ribs, Zak drew his six-shooter and peered into the dense trees. It might be a deer. They could sound mighty human-like.

He struck the gun's barrel against a wash-tub hanging on the wall. The sharp clank echoed. An animal would've scampered. Nothing moved, making it more likely he'd alerted a man who might now be pointing a weapon at him.

In a voice just above conversation level, he called out, "Horace, is that you?"

No answer.

Zak crouched ran around the next corner, gun poised, hammer cocked.

An outhouse stood at the edge of the woods, easy to identify by the crescent moon cut into the door. The door swung open and Horace came into view. When he spied Zak, he jumped back like he'd almost stepped on a snake. "What are you doing out here?"

Zak holstered his gun. "Maybe the same thing

you're doing."

Horace barked a laugh. "I used the last corn cob." He leaned in, squinting. "What happened to you? Don't tell me your new wife did that."

Zak touched the swelling on his face. "I ran into the door."

Horace chuckled under his breath. "Seems like you could think of a better excuse than that." He made to turn, then swung back around. "Where is that woman you're supposed to be guarding? Wasn't that the reason for the wedding, so you could keep an eye on her?"

Jeannie. That must have been her in the woods. She was making her escape. What a dope he was. Of course she'd try to get away. He'd explained to her the danger of trying to escape, that Clive would go after her, and he was an experienced tracker. He'd kill her when he found her.

The morning air was chilled, but sweat popped out on his forehead. He couldn't tell her the other reasons she shouldn't escape—reasons involving other people and higher stakes. "I left her in her room to give her some privacy."

"Privacy." Horace bellowed. "Since when does a wife want privacy from her husband?"

He had to get rid of Horace. "Go see for yourself. She'll be in her room." He pivoted toward the woods, ready to run.

"I'm here." The soft, feminine voice snapped his head back. Jeannie came along the path from the house with a milk pail swinging in one hand.

Horace leaned in as he passed Zak. "Better not let Clive know you're giving her privacy or he'll turn you into a widower before high noon."

"Jeannie and I will take care of the stock and get breakfast ready."

Horace sent a hard stare through them and stalked back to the house.

She had changed dresses. The rose plaid skirt and white shirtwaist made her appear older, or maybe it was because her hair was balled and pinned to the back of her head. The loose tendrils framing her face proved she hadn't taken much time to put her hair up.

"I have to milk Dolly," she said, holding the pail in front of her, as if he might demand an explanation.

"All right. I'll take the horses out." He followed her into the barn.

She entered the stall with the Guernsey cow and sat on the stool. Soon she had milk squirting into the pail with a rhythm that was almost musical.

He brought the first two horses out and retrieved some loose boards to make a latch for Jeannie's room. She did need some privacy. When he returned to Dolly's stall, Jeannie's murmuring stopped him. At first he thought she was talking to Dolly with her head leaning against the gentle cow's middle. Then he realized she was praying. And looking angelic.

Forcing his attention away from Jeannie, he

got all five horses settled in the corral before returning to the barn. Jeannie met him with the full pail in hand, her eyes squinting against the low sunrise.

"Let me get that for you." He shifted the wood to his left hand and held out his right.

"I can do it. I've been doing it all my life." Her grip on to the pail tightened.

She was amazingly strong for a woman. He took her to be no more than five-feet-four, but a lot of muscle was packed on her shapely form. Last night, he'd noticed how hard her biceps were. If her muscles were as large as a man's, she'd have him and his two despicable cohorts laid out flat and on their way to jail.

"What are you doing with the wood?" She referred to the four foot length of two-by-fours and the four smaller blocks he'd found in the barn.

"I'm going to set up a bar for your bedroom door so you'll...so you'll feel safer in there."

A slight smile curved her lips as she

relinquished the pail. "I have to pick the eggs."

He waited for her at the hen house. Her head appeared at the low entry, and when she rose, he noticed the pockets of her apron bulged.

"They gave me eight this morning. That's plenty for breakfast and to make a cake, with what I have in the pantry. Do you like chocolate cake?"

He hadn't had a chocolate cake since he'd left home. "Reckon I do." He fell into step with her. "Why didn't you escape when you had the chance?"

She sent him a startled glance, and he explained. "I heard you in the trees. You could have gotten away."

"I wouldn't get far without a horse, would I?" With a shrug, she continued on her way. "I got to thinking about what they might do to you if you'd let me get away. Even if I managed to get to town, who knows who would've gotten hurt."

"Trust me, Jeannie. My plan is best. When we get within sight of the Jackal's hideout, they won't bother to run after you. I'll make sure you escape."

"Who is this Jackal you speak of?"

"The big boss. He'll offer us sanctuary until...until the next job."

At the back door she gave him a skeptical look. "I haven't come to trust you yet, but I trust the Lord, and He tells me I should go along with you for now."

He left Jeannie to prepare the breakfast of ham and eggs and went to the parlor where Horace had dumped their things. He fished around in his saddle bag and retrieved two pairs of hand-cuffs and a length of chain about ten feet long. He hadn't told Jeannie yet, but he intended to chain her to the bed.

If Clive or Horace caught her trying to get away, it might be fatal. He figured the chain length would give her enough freedom to move around the room. The bar on her door would prevent anyone from coming in on her. He just hoped he could get the wooden slots nailed to the door facings before Clive stopped him.

He'd finished nailing the first nail in the last wood block when Jeannie screamed.

Chapter 6

Horace pushed his ugly, hairy face into Jeannie's, his sharp nails digging into her arms. "Where were you going, woman?"

She tried to twist from his grasp. Somewhere in the background she heard pounding footsteps.

"What are you doing?"

Horace swung around, dragging her with him. Zak stood before them, face sizzling red, pistol drawn. He slipped his arm around Jeannie's waist and pulled her to his side. "I told you not to touch my wife."

"She was trying to get away."

"I was not." She glanced up at Zak from under her lashes. His protective arm about her gave her courage. "I was just giving the cat some scraps...and he—" She shuddered. "He kicked the poor thing. There was no call for such meanness. I can forgive about anything but mistreating an innocent animal. Besides, I've been trying the hardest to tame that cat. It's been so lonely since Pa left." A sob broke through, and a tear ran down her cheek. The way she was going on, Zak probably thought her crazy.

Amazingly, he kissed her forehead. His week-long scruff brushed her skin, sending tingles down her spine.

"What's going on in here?"

Jeannie clung to Zak as Clive staggered into the room.

"Just a little misunderstanding, boss," Horace said.

Clive sat at the head of the table like he belonged there. He shifted his attention to Zak. "Where'd you get that shiner, boy?"

His snake eyes darted from Zak to Jeannie. She

recoiled, moving even closer to Zak. "Another misunderstanding." Zak's voice contained more steel than she'd heard before. Was he really standing up to Clive?

Surprisingly, Clive dismissed the matter. "Well I hope it was worth it for you." He looked down at his empty plate. "I feel better than I have in some time. Jeannie, I hope Horace told you I take my eggs soft scrambled. I can't tolerate ham or anything like that in the mornings. It sets my stomach on fire."

"The eggs are there under the napkin in the bowl, and I made you hot sweetened milk. It's easier on the stomach than coffee."

Clive snorted. "Is that right? You might convince me it's a good idea to take you with us after all."

Jeannie looked to Zak for approval. Did Clive mean he wouldn't be trying to kill her at every turn? The frown on Zak's face said he didn't trust Clive.

She ate what little she could swallow at the stove while the men consumed every crumb she served.

Zak was the first to push his chair back. "Jeannie and I are going out to the pasture. There's a fence down."

She sent a puzzled glance his way. She'd told him about the fence last night, but hadn't hoped she'd be allowed outside her prison. "Zak would you give me a few minutes to change into my working clothes?"

"Sure thing. It'll give me time to saddle our horses." Zak dropped in step behind her.

"Don't forget how much you have to lose, boy." Clive hurled the veiled threat after them.

Jeannie stopped in her tracks, and Zak almost plowed into her. He didn't even turn around to acknowledge Clive's remark. Side-stepping around her, he continued on toward the front door.

She scooted inside her bedroom before either of the men in the kitchen could stop her. Relief spread through her when she noticed the bar Zak had installed on her door. She dropped the board into its slots, and for the first time felt safe enough to change clothes.

As she pulled on Pa's old britches, the ones she used to do chores, she wondered what Zak would think. It didn't much matter. Ranch work could be mighty dangerous for a woman wearing a flowing dress.

She unbarred the door and slipped outside as quietly as possible. Zak was already waiting with the reins of Pat, her gilding, in one hand and his own horse in the other. Heat burned her cheeks as his gaze sweep over her, and she wasn't surprised to see one of his brow hitch.

"I hope you'll excuse the way I'm dressed, but this is my normal work clothes." She took Pat's reins and stepped into the stirrup.

He hoisted her into the saddle. "Don't bother me none. You lead the way."

Hooves pounded the ground as they made a

bee-line for the east pasture where she'd found the broken fence.

A few red steers grazed behind the fence. She counted them, relieved none had escaped yet.

Zak unhooked the roll of wire from his saddle and set to work.

"What do you want me to do?" she asked.

"Just stand there and watch. You shouldn't have to do this, Jeannie."

She'd be glad to watch him. He was a handsome man. His glossy hair glimmered in sunlight. His muscles bulged as he stretched the wire. "There's no one else to do it. You'll find most women out here have to turn their hands to whatever needs doing."

He turned from the fence and tipped his hat back on his head. After hooking the hammer on fence, he pierced her with a soul-searching glance and reached out to stroke her cheek. "It's not right, though. You're a beautiful woman, Jeannie. Have you been told that before?"

74

Heat crept up her neck. Did he think her beautiful? She automatically tried to smooth her skirt before realizing she wore britches. She wished she'd worn a dress. "No, never have."

He smiled. "That's not right either." Abruptly, he turned back to the job, and in half the time it would have taken her, finished securing the broken fence.

"Anything else out here that needs fixing? I don't know about you, but I'm not anxious to get back to the house."

No, she didn't want to get back to the house until those two evil men were gone. She shaded her eyes from the glare of the climbing sun. "We could talk, if you've a mind to, but let's get out of the sun." A lot needed to be said. A lot she wanted to know.

A bead of sweat already lined his brow, more from hard work than the heat, and he nodded to her suggestion. They walked across to a copse of trees about twenty yards away. Zak took his hat off and swiped his forehead with his shirtsleeve. She didn't have to prod him. "I guess you have a right to know what we're up against, Jeannie."

"How did you get mixed up in your step-pa's gang?" Anyone would know Zak didn't fit in. Even Clive must know. "What did he mean, you have a lot to lose?"

"Why does any man get mixed up in a gang? For the money—but I've got to prove myself first. The Jackal don't accept anyone in the gang except for murderers."

"Who's the Jackal?"

"The ring leader. The one who sets up the jobs and gets his men out of trouble if they get caught. I don't know much about him, and no one knows his real name. They say he's a well-respected judge with high level connections. None of his gangs have ever seen what he looks like. He always wears a mask. The only part of him anyone's ever seen is his eyes and hands. They say he washes his hands so much, the skin is raw and blistered."

With a mirthless chuckle, he added, "If only half the things said of the Jackal is true, he's probably infested with all sorts of demons."

If Zak believed that, didn't he know he was working for the devil too? Something told her Zak still held on to some of the faith his mother had taught him. "And you think the money is worth that?"

He drew in a deep breath, and she knew he wanted to avoid answering. "I have to meet the Jackal, Jeannie. I want to know what game he's playing. That's all I can tell you."

She threw Pat's reins over a low lying limb. "There's a fallen tree trunk over there where we can sit." She and Pa had often stopped here to eat their mid-day meal in the shade.

Their boots scrunched pine needles as she made for the ancient oak that had been lying on the ground for over a year, long enough for most of the bark to have fallen off. She found her favorite spot. Zak straddled the thicker end, giving him a good view of her.

They sat in the woodland silence only broken by the sparrows, wrens, and finches singing above them.

She hadn't missed the look of admiration he gave her. If the circumstances were different—if he were just a ranch hand—she'd have accepted his attention with giddy pleasure. But he was an outlaw. "I don't believe you joined up with your step-pa's gang because of money. You're strong and able. You could get a safer job."

"You're right about that, but I have to meet the big boss first, and that won't happen until I pass my test."

"What is the test?"

"That I kill someone." He said it so casually, a chill ran up her back.

She hugged herself. "Who?"

"In Clive's mind, anyone would do, but the Jackal is more discriminating. He insists it be someone who's a threat to the gang. He doesn't believe in wasting a bullet on someone who doesn't matter. That's what he says, anyway, but I think the less killing, the cheaper for him to get his thugs out of trouble. The way he thinks makes me believe he might be some big businessman who has the law in his pocket."

"He sounds despicable. Why would you want to have anything to do with him?" It made no sense to her. She sensed Zak had a good heart, that he actually hated Clive's debauchery. Why would he want to meet this outlaw leader?

"Oh, he is that, but there's some logic to his madness. Clive has his own mad reasons."

Zak twisted around on the log and stretched his long legs out in front. "Clive is playing a game too. He's promised to give me his portion of the loot, if I pass his test. If I prove he can trust me."

"What's wrong with him?"

"He has a cancer growing inside him, and he's going to die soon. He claims he's going to San Francisco to live out his last days, but he has another reason."

He plucked a pine needle off from a nearby limb and began chewing it. Staring at nothing. Pondering. "The Jackal gives a bonus to anyone who brings in a new gang member. That's why Clive brought me along."

"If he's going to die anyway, what does he want with a bonus?"

"He hasn't told me any of this, but he's heard of a surgeon in San Francisco who can cut out a cancer so it doesn't come back. Clive intends to use the bonus money he'll get for bringing in a new gang member to hire that surgeon. He intends to cheat death like he's cheated everyone else in his life."

"What's Clive's test for you?" When Zak didn't answer, she knew the answer. "He wants you to kill me, doesn't he?"

She got up, unable to look into his handsome face for the moment. Zak shot after her and was by her side before she realized it. He pulled her to him. "I'm not going to let anyone hurt you, Jeannie. I swear if it comes to it, I'll take the bullet for you. Believe me, I'd never harm you."

Forcing her glance to his eyes, she found a different kind of tenderness there. Something deeper than concern of one person for another. He bit the side of his lower lip. "You know most men have a picture in their mind about who the perfect woman is, the one they'd like to marry. When I first saw you, I thought you might be that woman, then when you lit into me like a wildcat, I knew you were. You have all the beauty and courage I've ever dreamed of, Jeannie."

Emotion caught in her throat. She wanted to believe him. A part of her melted, a part of her resisted. She'd had dreams too, dreams she'd someday hear those beautiful words he'd spoken to her, but never had she imagined they'd come from an outlaw who contemplated murder. True, it wasn't her murder, but it was still dangerous to encourage his feelings for her. "But it's not just

Clive. The big boss expects you to kill someone who'd endanger the gang, and I'd fit that requirement."

His eyes turned hard. "I do intend to kill someone who endangers the gang—but not you. I'm going to kill Clive."

She wasn't really surprised by the venom in his voice. "He's already a member," she reminded him.

"He's a double-crosser."

The hatred in his eyes told her he meant it. But killing someone, even someone as evil as Clive was wrong.

She pressed her palms against his chest. "We could both escape, Zak. We could ride away and they couldn't catch us. The posse wouldn't recognize you if you were with me. We could go to Medicine Bow and find my pa. He'd help you get away from the gang."

Alarm showed in his features. "I'm not going to involve you and your pa in this mess."

"But you don't have to do this. You don't

belong in this gang. I know you don't. You're a good man." She patted his chest to remind him he had a heart.

He caught her by the wrists, shaking his head. "No, my plan is the best way, Jeannie. We'll clear out of here Friday after I find out where the posse went. We'll have to go along with Clive and Horace until I learn the location of the Jackal's lair, then I'll find the nearest stage and put you on it." His eyes took on the look of a man who doubted his own words.

What about her when he rode to town in search of information about the posse? She'd be left to the mercies of Clive and Horace. Hadn't he thought of that?

She shook her head. "No, no, no. I don't want to go back to the house while those men are there. Please, Zak. You've said Clive wants me dead. If you refuse to do his bidding, he'll kill me."

"He trusts me right now, but I may have to be a little rough with you. I'm going to have to chain you to your bed when I have to go out, but you'll be able to move about the room and put the bar in place so no one can burst in on you."

Chained? She shuddered as hope sank like a capsized ship. Zak couldn't save her. It was folly to trust anyone but herself and God. "I have chores to do. My garden needs weeding."

"I'll do the chores, weed the garden. Do you have anything to keep you occupied in your room during the day? I'll make sure I'm with you while you're cooking."

Did she have anything to do? She'd almost forgotten. "I have to finish crocheting Rose's cloak. She's my friend, ordered to bed since she had a fall. The cloak will keep her shoulders warm so she can sit up in bed. Anyway, I promised her I'd bring it to her on Sunday. I always go visit Rose and Willie and Pauline on Sunday." She pressed two fingers against her lips. "If I don't show up, she'll send Willie to check on me. What if the gang's still here? They'll kill Willie. That can't happen."

"Relax. I'll take the cloak to your friend when I go to town Friday."

Would that be time enough to finish the cloak? At least five or six inches waited to be crocheted. With nothing to do but sit in her room, there'd be more than enough time. "How long will you be gone Friday? I'll have to come out of my room to prepare meals."

Zak lifted his hat and scratched his head. His frown indicated he hadn't thought of that. "You can fix a big pot of stew. That'll hold the varmints until I return, and I won't be gone all day." His gaze held hers for a long moment, then the corners of his mouth creased in a grin that would charm the living daylights out of any woman between the ages of nine and ninety.

He nodded toward the horses. "We'd better be getting back or Clive will send Horace after us."

Her boots crunched the ground in hurried steps, Zak following close behind. She pulled Pat's reins from the branch where he was tethered.

While Zak fussed with his horse's leathers, she swung into the saddle and wheeled her gelding around. Shoving her knees into Pat's sides as hard as she ever had, she held on as the surprised horse sprang into a rearing gallop.

Despite the futility of her action, Jeannie guided the racing horse toward the road leading to town. Thundering hooves, hers and Zak's horse, pounded the ground as she fought to control a horse unused to such treatment. She didn't even reach the road before Zak pulled up beside her and yanked the reins from her.

When they were fully stopped, Jeannie glanced up to find eyes darkened with anger, boring into her. Frustrated tears welled, and she swiped them with the back of her hand.

"What are you trying to do? Get us killed?"

She flinched under the rancor in his voice and dropped her head to stare at the saddle horn. "I'd hoped...just maybe...you'd let me escape."

His sigh softened his tone. "I wish I could,

Jeannie, but Clive would kill me if I let you go. Do you want that?"

A curl escaped her pins and fell on her forehead as she shook her head. "No, of course not. We could both escape. They wouldn't follow us to town."

"Yes, they would. Besides, what waits for me in town, Jeannie? The hangman's noose."

A protest formed on her lips but died before she spoke. For all she knew, the posse waited for Zak and all the gang's crimes would be leveled against him, regardless of whether he'd committed them or not, simply because of his association with the gang.

Lord, provide an escape for both of us.

She stiffened her spine and moistened her lips. A new plan formed in her mind—one that suited her a lot more than Zak's. It might not only save her, but hopefully save Zak as well.

Chapter 7

Sun streaked a cloudless sky as they rode up to the house. Zak couldn't avoid the irony of the situation. A beautiful, bright, ordinary world existed outside, while on the other side of those walls, lay darkness.

Jeannie fixed a noon meal of ham sandwiches while Zak set up the apparatus to keep her chained to her bed. It was a cruel thing to do, but necessary. If she had the chance to escape, she would. Not only would Clive not allow her to keep the door barred without some guarantee she couldn't escape, but Zak couldn't risk it. He wanted to set her free. Badly. But other lives depended on the secrecy of his plans.

Clive and Horace grumbled at the kitchen table. Each time they yelled expletives, Zak cringed. He wouldn't have noticed before, but Jeannie was in there, serving those yahoos. She shouldn't have to hear this filth, be exposed to this evil.

They were filthy inside and out. He'd insist all three men take a bath this afternoon, even if Horace squawked. Maybe a little cleanliness would help their dispositions. For sure, it would help Zak, and who knew how long it would be before they'd get another chance?

Clive expected Jeannie to wash their clothes, but Zak would do the laundry. The light breeze would have their clothes dry by sundown. While the clothes dried, he'd weed Jeannie's vegetable garden.

As he'd promised her, he'd take care of the chores and leave her safely in her room crocheting her friend's cloak. He'd much rather spend the time with her, but she was a temptation. It was hard enough lying there on the floor of her bedroom at night.

Clive's rants pulled his attention to the kitchen. "I told you I couldn't eat ham."

Zak dropped his hammer and rushed to Jeannie's aid, in case she needed it.

She stooped over the table, cutting bread. Another curse had the bread knife toppling from her hand. "That's all I have. I could cook some cornmeal mush." She retrieved the knife and went on cutting without looking up.

Zak admired how she refused to allow Clive to rattle her.

"No, I don't want any infernal cornmeal mush. That's all we had out on the trail."

Zak took the knife from Jeannie, and she glanced up expectantly. "Why don't you fix him some more of those soft scrambled eggs?"

"If I do, I won't have any eggs for the cake."

"Who cares? Fix the eggs." Clive's eyes had

sunk in their sockets. It wasn't going to be a good day for him, and when it wasn't a good day for Clive, it wasn't a good day for anyone.

"We'll have to forego the cake today," Zak said. "You'll need to stay in your room most of the day anyway."

"No cake? Why do we have to eat what you do, Clive?" Horace asked.

"Because I said so. Get those eggs on, gal, and fix some more of that vanilla milk."

As soon as she'd finished with Clive's lunch, Zak took the sandwiches he'd made and put his arm around her shoulder. Sitting here with Clive and Horace was enough to spoil anyone's appetite. He dragged her along to the bedroom.

He shoved the sandwiches in her hand and barred the door.

She gave him a searching glance. "What's wrong?"

He rubbed his mouth with the back of his hand. "I forgot to tell you Clive gets nastier as the day wears on. Best you stay in here."

She handed him his sandwich and went to the rocker. "That's fine with me. I really appreciate the bar on the door. I know they could break it down if they wanted to, but it makes me feel safer."

"Yeah, it's better." But not good enough. He lowered himself on the edge of the bed.

For the next minute silence reigned as they ate, he in a few bites, she nibbling around the edges. He poured water from the pitcher in a glass and took a long swig. After refilling the glass, he offered it to Jeannie.

"Bread is getting a little dry." Her chuckle was a delightful sound after the tension in the other room. "I ought to make more."

"That'll have to wait until supper. As I told you, you need to stay in here this afternoon."

He saw her glance travel to the chain lying across the end of the bed. "Chained?"

"Sorry, but yeah."

"You won't ride off and leave me like that, will

you? I can't help the fear you'd all leave me chained, and I might have to chew off my hand. I've heard of animals doing that."

Did she really think he'd be that cruel? He got up to kneel down beside her chair. "An animal caught in a trap." Her doe-like eyes probed his. "That's the way I'll feel."

"I won't leave you, Jeannie, until you're safe."

"You're asking me to trust you a lot."

"Yeah, I am."

"But what if there's a fire? I'll be trapped."

"I'll be close enough to smell the smoke. I'll get you out if there's a fire."

"You're going to town day after tomorrow."

He smiled and brushed back the tendril resting on her cheek. "I won't chain you when I go to town. Just don't let those other polecats know."

"I don't know that I can trust you completely, Zak, but I trust God. I've been praying hard and I have a peace about it. God is going to save me from this somehow...and He's going to save you too, Zak."

Chapter 8

His laugh was derisive as he got to his feet. "I'm beyond God's help, Jeannie."

She grabbed his hand. "No, you're not. You believe in Jesus, you said so yourself."

He squeezed her hand. "The demons believe in Jesus."

"But only because they live in the spirit world and can't deny Him. You believe in faith."

"I can't expect Jesus to save me when I plan on killing a man, even a low-down man like Clive."

Jeannie sprang from the rocker, leaving it swaying. "You don't have to kill him, Zak. He's so close to death now, God will probably take care of the job before you can."

His green eyes darkened to the shade of a forest at dusk. "No, I have to do it. I have to kill him or I wouldn't be able to live with myself."

Her sigh shook her whole body. "Will you stay a little while and read to me while I crochet? I have to finish this cloak for Rose.

I can't stay long. I've determined those two thugs and I are going to take a bath and wash our clothes. I'm sure you're tired of smelling us polecats."

She hadn't been bothered by Zak's smell at all. Yes, it was earthy, but he carried the scent of the woods and horse and leather. A pleasant combination. The other two were something else. Horace's sour smell almost nauseated her, and Clive carried the scent of death for many different reasons. She doubted a bath would change that.

"What do you want me to read?"

She was busy counting her stitches and almost missed his question. "All I have is the Bible." She pointed to the big black book lying atop the highboy. "Please read in the Psalms. When I'm afraid, I find praising God calms me best. I would sing if I could carry a tune, but since I can't, I read the Psalms.

He laughed. "I haven't read the Bible since Ma died, so don't be surprised if I sound off-key."

She knew enough of Zak's story to know he'd hardened his heart against God after his mother's death, and she hoped the scriptures would help him as much as her.

Soon his voice had her mesmerized. Hearing the words spoken always moved her more than just reading, especially when it was spoken by a strong, male voice. Zak sounded even better than Pa.

Her crochet hook flashed in and out as she added stitches, relaxing under the comfort of the Psalms. She missed a stitch when someone pounded on the door.

Horace's gruff voice came from the other side.

"Zak, you need to get outa there. I got the tub ready."

With a sigh, Zak close the Bible and returned it to its place. He came to her with the chain. The clinking sound of the metal links hit her like a splash of cold water. "Sorry I have to do this, but it's long enough to allow you to move around the room. You bar the door as soon as I leave."

Being able to lock others out brought little comfort to her as the chain snapped snug around her waist. Zak attached the other end of the chain with the second pair of cuffs and locked it around two rods of the iron bedstead. She was as secured as a prisoner in the dock.

After she'd slipped the two-by-four in place, she went, not back to the rocker, but to her little writing desk. Being situated at the far corner of the room, it took up almost all of the chain. In fact, she'd have to lean over instead of sitting, but that didn't matter. She retrieved her ink pot and pen and a half-page of stationery.

She dipped the pen and, stooping over the paper, began writing. Having rehearsed the words all night as she'd lain in the darkness, they flowed from the ink.

Dear Rose, I am in danger...

She explained the situation, asking that Willie go to town and get the law. She repeated that Willie should not come to the ranch because the men were dangerous, and there were three of them.

Would they go looking for Zak? Hopefully, the law would get here before he returned or he'd see what was going on and hide out. After rereading the words, she bit her lip and added, *the man who brought you the cloak is helping me, don't tell the sheriff about him.*

That might sound strange, but it was as good as she could do to protect Zak. She folded the paper into a small square and took it back to where her cloak lay draped over the rocker's arm.

Rose had requested Jeannie crochet hidden

pockets on the inside of the armhole slits so she'd have a place to tuck her handkerchiefs. Zak, being a man, wouldn't even know the cloak had pockets, but Rose would look for the pockets right away and find the note. At least that's what Jeannie prayed. This was her only hope. It was up to the Lord now.

Of course Willie would leave as soon as Rose found the note, he'd be right behind Zak, but Zak wasn't going by the road, so it was unlikely either man would see the other. Jeannie reasoned, if the lawmen came immediately, they should arrive by afternoon.

Please, Lord, delay Zak until after then. She continued crocheting the last rows of the cloak.

She stored the cloak in the top drawer of the highboy, and got out the half-finished baby bonnet for Rose's baby, working on it until Zak came to get her to prepare supper. He'd changed clothes to a checked blown and white shirt and jeans. One whiff told her he'd used the scented lye soap. He'd trimmed his beard and combed his hair.

He must know she found him attractive, because he smiled every time he caught her looking at him, which was a lot. It was hard to quit looking at him.

The next day, while Zak took care of the chores, Jeannie holed up in her room crocheting, but she got up frequently, pulled to the room's small window. She watched Zak working in the garden, tending the horses, bringing Dolly in from her pasture, and a hundred other tasks that called his attention. From the open barn doors, she saw him mucking out the stalls.

This man wasn't an outlaw. He was a rancher.

Clive and Horace stayed indoors, playing cards, talking low, planning some future evil, she supposed.

Zak came to her room late. He read some more of the Psalms as she crocheted. She found herself telling him about her girlhood, her hopes for the future—if she had a future—things she'd never told anyone, not even Pa or Rose.

He didn't like to talk about his past, but she gathered his childhood had been happy before his pa died, then turned bad when his ma married Clive.

She knew better to ask him again to escape with her, but she tried one more time. "After you've seen the Jackal and settled whatever you have to settle, will you leave the gang for good?"

He gave her a look that peered into her soul. "I've been thinking on it."

"I would be so happy. Will you let me know if you do?"

"I promise you I will, Jeannie. It would make me happy just to see you happy."

He hadn't exactly said he'd leave the gang, but it was enough for her to hug to her and dream about. It would do for now.

Chapter 9

A moaning like a dying animal drifted across Zak's dream. A soft voice called his name. The fingers of sleep held him to his pallet, and his half-conscious brain told him it was a dream.

"Zak." A real voice. Someone shook his shoulder. A real hand. His eyes snapped opened, and Jeannie's pretty features came into focus in the dusky light.

Panic jerked him upright. "What's wrong?

"That noise—what is it?"

Zak had no trouble hearing the groan that grew into a muffled shriek. Groans and shrieks followed like stormy waves crashing on the rocks.

Zak rolled across the floor and put his ear to the space under the door. A few moments later, he sprang to his feet. "Nothing to get upset about. That's just Clive. He has good nights and bad. Guess this is a bad one."

Concern twisted Jeannie's features as she pressed her ear against the door. "Sounds like he's in torment."

Zak couldn't squeeze out one drop of sympathy for Clive. "I expect he is. Go back to bed, Jeannie. I'll stuff the blanket under the door, and you'll hardly hear it."

Clive let out a shattering groan that made Zak's gut roil even with all the years of hate he'd stored up for the old man.

Staring at the ceiling, Jeannie pressed her fingers to her temple. "Old Aunt Jergins had a stomach tumor. The pain got fearsome sometimes, even after she'd taken all the laudanum the doctor allowed. Ma and I made up a poultice and plastered her stomach with it, and the pain lessened a lot."

Zak could only gap at her. Would she seriously consider doctoring that lowdown scoundrel?

As if she'd read his mind, Jeannie met his stare. "The poor old dear died anyway, but she claimed we helped her more than the doctor. I could make a poultice for Clive."

Draping one hand over her shoulder, he eased her to the bed. "You do know that man is planning to kill you?"

"I do know, Zak, but I...I can't listen to his suffering when I know I might could help." She turned to him and pierced him with a pleading look. "Let me do it, Zak. While I'm fixing the poultice, you go see if he'll let me apply it."

She was a better Christian than he was. Who was he kidding? He couldn't claim to be a Christian at all. He had too much hate wadded up inside him.

He rubbed his fist across his nose. "All right, come on." He unbarred the door and held it open for her.

Leaving Jeannie hustling around the kitchen, he rapped on Clive's bedroom door with more reluctance than entering a bear's den.

"Whadda ya want?"

Clive propped up against the bed's headboard, eyes closed, clutching his stomach.

Zak lifted the lantern he'd brought to get a better look. He kicked debris out of his way on his way to the bedside. The room was a mess. The bedside table covered with half-smoked cheroots. The whole place stunk like an opium den. He set the lantern on a chest of drawers, and the light set ghostly shadows dancing in the walls.

"How're you doing, Clive?"

"A fool question, but I'm going to hang on as long as I have to." His groaning undercut the confidence of his words. Clive's bearded face scrunched in agony for several seconds, and when he relaxed, he sent a sharp look toward Zak. "You changed your mind about the girl, haven't you?"

Zak didn't have to hedge his answer. "No, nothing's changed. I'll get rid of her at the appointed time." He'd get rid of her by letting her escape, but Clive couldn't know that. Nevertheless, he didn't underestimate how shrewd the old man was.

"You haven't developed a caring for her?"

Zak twisted his mouth and shook his head. "No more than I'd care for any saloon gal, and it's like you said, they'll believe any lie you tell them."

To accentuate his point, he leaned down and lowered his voice as if he feared Jeannie might hear. "I've told her I'm getting out of the gang after this job, and we'll get married in the church."

Clive laughed and that led to a coughing fit that had him howling again.

Jeannie slipped into the room holding a large bowl filled with some fowl smelling stuff that battled with the stench already pervading the room.

She stopped just inside the room. "Did he

agree?"

Zak could barely hear her above Clive's coughing. "Clive, Jeannie has a poultice that's said to help people with stomach tumors. Will you try it?"

Apparently Clive hadn't heard her come into the room. His eyes shot open and darted from Zak to Jeannie. The cheesecloth covered bowl she held shook as she stepped toward Clive's bed. "I can't promise it'll help, but I've seen it relieve one patient."

Clive surprised Zak by lifting his shirt and baring his extended stomach. "Go ahead, couldn't hurt more than it does now."

Jeannie flipped the bowl, catching the glob in the cheesecloth. She nodded for Zak to take the bowl. As the poultice hovered over Clive, Zak's muscles tightened, ready to jump in between Jeannie and Clive, whose pistol rested beside his hand.

"It'll burn for a few seconds," she said. "But if

it's going to reduce the pain, you'll notice right away." She plopped the poultice over Clive's stomach and pressed it into place, covering the whole area.

Clive flinched as his skin came in contact with the poultice, then his chest swelled with a deep breath.

Both Jeannie and Zak watched, waiting for a reaction, ready for anything. The old man lay as quiet as death while the wall clock ticked in the silent room.

Zak could stand it no more. "Does it help any?"

Clive grunted. "Still hurts...but yeah, it's better."

Jeannie stepped back. "It'll last about an hour. Maybe you can get some sleep now."

"That'll hold me, I guess. I can take some more opium by then. Much obliged, Missy."

If Zak hadn't heard it, he wouldn't have believed it. Clive had actually thanked someone. He snagged the lantern and followed Jeannie back

109

to her bedroom. But sleep evaded him the rest of the night. Tomorrow might be his last full day with Jeannie. That was both good and bad. His feelings for her had deepened. Maybe desire clouded his thinking. Not a good thing. He had to have all his wits about him.

The most dangerous part of the operation lay ahead. He had two ways to go. Either the posse could be found, in which case, they'd have to take Clive and Horace alive. If that happened, Zak might have to pretend to fight on Clive and Horace's side. They could all be killed—including Jeannie. He'd try his best to avoid that kind of confrontation. If the posse wasn't around, they'd go on to see the Jackal as planned—Jeannie included.

The only thing giving him solace was the fact that Clive knew Jeannie could make a poultice that helped his pain. For that reason, he'd be more willing to keep her alive. It would take all day to think out the strategy. He'd play out each step in his mind while he did the ranch chores. One mistake could spell disaster.

As soon as the first streaks of light appeared, Zak chained Jeannie to her bedstead before he left to do the milking. He released her for breakfast, then secured her to the chain again, making certain she had room to reach and bar the door behind him.

She didn't like it, nor did he, but she could at least spend the day crocheting her friend's cloak without fear of being disturbed—or so he hoped.

He didn't tell her, but it was quite possible he wouldn't see her again after tomorrow morning. Too much could happen, and if it would put her in danger, he wouldn't return at all.

Since it hadn't rained for a while, he hauled water to her garden and tilled the ground to keep the weeds down. Her spinach was producing nicely and the early peas would soon be ready for harvesting.

Zak had always wanted to be a farmer or a

rancher. He enjoyed the work. The animals. The soil between his fingers. After all this was over, he'd take his money and buy a piece of land somewhere, maybe somewhere around here.

Her horses, Pat and Ned, had gotten used to him, and in the afternoon before the air turned chill, he took them one after another out for a ride around the property. It was a beautiful land with the mountains in the west and hilly grassland in the east. Too hilly for farming, maybe, but perfect for cattle. Yes, it was time to find a small farm or ranch like this and settle down. If God was forgiving enough to give him another chance, he wanted to share his life with Jeannie. If she would have him. He couldn't imagine another woman in all the world he'd rather grow old with.

Would he return? Could he win her? Would she be willing to forgive him and marry him in truth?

The day passed quickly. Jeannie unbarred the door after he announced himself, and he unchained her, since it was time for supper. He wouldn't chain her tomorrow.

The meal passed in tense silence, each man seemingly concentrating on his own plans. It was better that Jeannie not know what those plans were, but Zak suspected she knew the end was at hand.

She prepared another poultice for Clive. He snatched it from her, declaring he knew what to do with it, and went straight to his bedroom, then turned back at the door. "Remember to get an early start tomorrow, boy, and scout the edge of town first. No one saw you at that hold-up, so you shouldn't cause any suspicion. Just remember how much depends on this for you—and her." He disappeared inside.

Before Zak and Jeannie could escape to the bedroom, Horace called from the parlor. "Looky what I found yesterday." He held up a guitar. "How about playing for us. I'm tired of playing solitaire and I ain't sleepy."

Zak started to refuse, but Jeannie took the guitar. "This is Pa's. Do you play, Zak?"

"A little."

She held it out to him. "Please play a little. I've finished the cloak, and the night's early."

"You heard your wife," Horace said. "Play something with a little life in it. This place is as dead as a tomb. How about *Camptown Races*?"

Zak took the instrument and strummed. He began with the old campfire tunes that had Horace stomping his big foot and Jeannie clapping. "You play beautifully, Zak."

He played chords at random. Maybe some Stephen Foster ballads would please her.

She sat on the edge of her chair on the far wall, probably to keep as much distance between her and Horace as possible. From the expression on her face, she'd forgotten the raunchy outlaw. All her attention riveted on Zak, making his insides quiver.

A little smile lifted the corners of her slightly

parted lips, and the lamplight cast a halo on unadorned hair cascading in waves to her waist.

Without realizing it, the music flowed from his heart.

"I dream of Jeannie with the light brown hair, born like a vapor on the soft summer air."

And that was exactly how she'd come into his life. One moment he was dead inside, filled with hatred and bent on revenge. The next—she appeared, thawing the edges of his heart, making him believe he could care again.

At this point in time, all the trouble of the past few days disappeared. He might as well be calling on his lady love, entertaining her with the intention of marrying her someday. She must have read his mind, since she blushed and dropped her glance to her lap as he sang.

"I long for Jeannie—"

The door to Clive's room slammed open. "Stop than infernal caterwauling."

Jeannie bounded from her chair as if shot, and

Clive stabbed her with a hard look before shooting it to Zak. "I can't sleep with all this noise. You better get to bed early, boy. Can't take a chance on over-sleeping."

Zak lay the guitar aside and got to his feet. Clive's meaning was as clear as a mountain stream. He had no business singing love songs to a woman he would have to murder. He all but pushed Jeannie into her bedroom and bolted the door.

Jeannie started fixing Zak's pallet. "Clive is right about one thing. You do have to get to sleep early."

She snapped the blanket he used for bed covers, and he caught it in the air.

A question lifted her feathered brows.

"Jeannie, I'm going to sleep in the barn tonight."

"Why?"

How could he tell her why? Because he didn't trust himself to lie in this room with her another night, listening to her prayers, watching how the moon beams played across her lovely face while she slept.

So close. So far away.

He draped the chain around her waist and locked it with a snap. "I hate doing this, but I can't trust that you wouldn't try to escape in the night. I know I would."

"You can't trust me, yet you ask me to trust you."

"I know, but you'll understand soon, or I hope you do." He took a step back. "I'll be in for breakfast shortly after the cock crows in the morning."

"I still don't understand how you can care for me—and I know you do—but you leave me like this."

"I'm not sure I understand either." He glanced to the ceiling and blew a lung full of air through closed lips. "I'm not going to chain you tomorrow, but you have to promise me you won't try to make a run for it. It's all the excuse Clive or Horace would need to—" He lifted her chin with two fingers. "Promise."

"All right. I promise, but I will keep the door barred."

"I think Clive will leave you alone. Since you fixed him those poultices he sees you as an advantage. He keeps people around who serve a purpose—his purpose."

"And tonight?"

He slipped the pistol from his holster and laid it on the highboy. "If either of them try to break in on you, use this. I'll hear the gunfire and come to you."

She grabbed hold of his forearm. "Don't go, Zak. I'm afraid when you're not near."

He stared at her slender fingers gripping his shirtsleeve. When his gaze met hers, he found tears welling in her eyes. The scent of her intoxicated him, intensifying his need. Nerves lodged in his throat, and he coughed them back.

Knowing he shouldn't, he stroked her cheek,

soft as a rose petal, and wiped a tear with his thumb. "You're so lovely—inside and out."

Her lips parted as more tears fell, and he pulled her into his arms. She came as eagerly and as trusting as a new bride. He kissed her salty cheek with tender-laced passion.

"Come back to Jesus, Zak. You're not very far." Her words fell like honey on his ears, but also reminded him of his mission. How could he expect Jesus to take him back when he intended to get revenge by murdering a man, even a man as despicable as Clive?

He held her by the shoulders, putting some space between them. "This is what I do promise you, Jeannie. If I make it through all this, I'll return to you. Wherever I go, I'll find you again." His throat was raw. "Don't you go marrying anyone else."

Her small balled fist went to her mouth as drops fell from wet lashes.

He kissed her forehead and took two steps

backward, finding the door knob. "Bar the door after me. I'll see you in the morning."

Then he was gone.

Chapter 10

Jeannie lay wide awake when the rooster crowed. She'd slept fitfully throughout the long night, praying between dozes.

Not wasting any time, she sprang from the bed and washed her face. Donning a fresh apron, she turned to face the day, whatever it brought.

The only sound that greeted her was Horace's roof-rattling snores. If only Clive would sleep late. She'd leave enough breakfast on the stove for them and maybe they would leave her alone—until help came.

She'd just pulled the biscuits from the oven when Zak came through the back door.

"Smells mighty good," he said, sliding into his regular chair as if this were just another day. Like he was her husband come in from the chores, hungry for breakfast.

If only that could be.

His hair, still wet from his wash clung to his forehead in clumps. He hadn't trimmed his beard and it shadowed his face. He wore a clean, tan shirt with jeans and black leather vest that matched his Stetson. The wound under his eye was healing, though purple and yellow streaks still marred his face.

She served the bacon, eggs, and biscuits with apple butter, taking advantage of his attention to the food to savor a long look at him. His vest and hat and boots were of high quality leather, made by a master leather craftsman. That belied his claim he needed to meet up with the Jackal simply because he needed the money. He wasn't poor. What was he hiding from her? And why?

He slathered apple butter on his biscuit and

glanced up at her. "Have any coffee this morning?"

She seemed to come to. "Oh, of course." With a dishcloth protecting her hand from the hot handle, she took the pot from the back of the stove and poured it into a mug. After adding a couple of teaspoons of sugar—the way he liked it—she stirred the coffee and set it before him.

"You going to eat?" he asked.

Anxiety filled her stomach. She could eat nothing. "I'll take a biscuit with me to eat in my room—after you leave."

"Hadn't you better be on your way, Zak?" Horace's question made her jump.

Horace passed the table, giving a long gander at the food. "Leave some for me." He went on out the back door, presumably on his way to the outhouse.

They didn't have long.

Zak took a long swig of his coffee and wiped his mouth. "I better go on now."

"Oh, I have to get the cloak." She scurried to

her room and returned with the cloak draped over outstretched arms.

"That's mighty pretty, Jeannie. You do good work."

"I wanted to make it in a fresh, spring color, but that's all the yarn I had."

He held it against his shirt. "Matches my shirt. Maybe someday you can make me a scarf out of the same yarn. Be nice for next winter."

She tried to read sincerity in his eyes, that he did intend to return so she could give him a scarf for next winter. But the teasing look he gave her was only meant to relieve tension—hers and his.

"Better be going. Try not to worry too much. Go ahead and lock yourself in your room. Don't come out for anything, even if they threaten to tear down the door. It'll take them awhile to do that." He covered the distance to the front door in a few long strides. "And use that gun if you have to."

She dogged his heels on out to the porch, down the steps. "You know where my friend lives?"

She'd already told him, but wanted to delay him as much as possible.

He turned and nodded. "Yeah, I know exactly where to go. Just off the main road. That's why we didn't stop off there when we were running from the posse."

"What if you find the posse?"

"Then we'll have to lay low for a while longer, I expect." He untied the reins of the waiting horse and climbed into the saddle. "It'll be up to Clive."

She stretched her hand to grab the edge of his saddle, reaching on tip-toe. "Be careful."

His hand held the back of her head as he lowered his face to hers and planted a knee-buckling kiss on her lips. "You too. Be praying."

What else could she do?

Back in her room, Jeannie paced. Had she sent him to his death? The law was looking for him, too. They might apprehend Zak first or some vigilante might shoot him.

She shook the doubts away. It was folly to

speculate. Faith called for keeping one's mind on God's promises. She got the Bible down and thumbed through the pages. When needing to be reassured, she always went to the Gospels.

Be of good cheer. I have overcome the world.

The minutes and hours ticked by. She went back and forth from the window, straining her eyes for any sign of activity, then to the door, straining her ears for any conversation between Clive and Horace.

Mercifully, they didn't come to her to prepare a noon meal, which seemed strange after she thought of it. What were they up to?

She went back to pacing, and in mid-stride, picked up the sound of distant hoof beats.

Someone was coming. The posse? But she detected only one horse.

Had Zak returned? *Please God, no.* That meant something was wrong.

Willie? The worst possible thing that could happen. No, she'd made it clear in her message it was too dangerous for Willie to come—and Willie wasn't overly courageous. A good husband to Rose. A wonderful father. But not courageous enough to run into danger.

That's something Zak would do.

Her heart was pounding so hard, she feared she'd faint. She dropped to the slit of light under the door and pressed her ear to the opening.

The horse stopped. Footsteps scuffled in the parlor. Men cursed and whispered. A knock jarred the door.

Hard raps against her bedroom door had her ear ringing. "Open up, gal. Right now."

Fear lodged in her throat as she rose to her feet. Zak had warned her not to open the door.

"Open up if you don't want me to blast this fellow to kingdom come—and you after him."

The visitor wasn't Zak, or Clive wouldn't be acting this way. She sent a backward glance to the pistol lying where Zak left it. No, she couldn't confront both Clive and Horace, even if she had the nerve to shoot them. They'd just take the weapon away from her.

With Clive still banging, she lifted the bar and cracked the door. Those evil black eyes bored into her, then the outlaw's claw of a hand dug into her forearm, pulling her out into the parlor. Rapping sounded at the front door like a woodpecker in a frenzy.

Clive dragged her to the door, his pistol drawn. "Open it and find out what he wants and get rid of him. One false move and it'll be your last."

Terror numbed her, making it difficult to slide the bolt.

The man standing on the other side of the threshold stretched a brown handlebar moustache with a smile. "Ma'am, you be Miss Baylor?"

Her tongue stuck to the roof of her mouth. "Y...yes."

"I was on the cattle drive with your pa. He asked me to stop by and tell you, he won't be back until early next week. Didn't want you to worry."

"Th...thank you."

The man doffed his hat and pivoted on his boot heel. She closed the door, glad that pa wouldn't be back before these outlaws vacated the premises.

Gunfire made her jump. Her wide startled eyes found the source. Clive holstered his still smoking six-gun. Horace had the curtain pulled all the way back and she caught sight of the visitor sprawled in the yard by his horse.

"Why'd you do that, boss?" Horace voiced her own question. "He was gonna leave."

"You idiot. That was one of the posse. I didn't recognize him myself until he was walking away. One of his shoulders slumped more than the other. Oh, I remember well. Go check out back." Clive whipped out a spy-glass from his coat pocket and stepped out onto the porch.

Stunned fear glued Jeannie to the floor. How could anyone kill another man, shoot him in the back, like that? If the man really was from the posse, Rose must have found her note in the cloak and sent Willie to alert the sheriff. But why would one man come alone? Hadn't she explained in her note how dangerous these men were?

Both Clive and Horace returned within seconds. "He was alone, but they'll come looking."

"Might be hiding in the woods," Horace said.

"The gunshot would've brought 'em out if they were." Clive's gaze lit on Jeannie as if he just noticed she was still there. "Get back to your room, gal."

She didn't need to be told twice. As if escaping torment, she made a dash for her room and started to put the bar in place when Clive called out. "Keep it unlatched."

It didn't matter. Being locked in afforded little real protection. What she really wanted to do was run. If only she could crawl out the window. But it was up too high and too small. Even her slender form might get stuck.

She left the door cracked to listen to what was going on.

"I'll start getting our stuff together," Horace said.

"No, I'll do that. You go back in the woods a piece and dig a grave for that fellow. When the rest of 'em ride up, I don't want 'em finding the body. If they don't find nothing here, it might buy us some time. And while you're at it, make the hole big enough for two."

"For two? You not taking the girl with us? What about Zak?"

"Zak'll have to find his own way, and the girl'll drag us down."

A grave for two. It took Jeannie a few seconds for the full impact to hit. Her mouth went dry and her pulse kicked up as...

"Whatcha going to tell Zak?"

"We don't have time to think about that now. Get outta here. I'll bring her on out when I get us packed up. I'll kill her at the hole you dig. Don't want nobody finding blood in the house."

Horace's heavy boots stomped toward the kitchen.

Drained of all strength, Jeannie fell back against the door. She clutched hands already raw from the wringing. If that devil out there thought she would just march to her own grave, he had another think coming. She'd fight him every step of the way. Her glance fell on Zak's pistol.

Too late.

She stumbled backward as the door flew open. "Get out here and scramble me up what's left of the eggs. We're leaving, and I need one good meal before we go."

Jeannie hugged the wall to get around him without touching. She dashed to the kitchen and got out the skillet. If he'd just turn his head for a second, she'd slam the skillet on it. But he kept an unblinking glare on her every move.

One of the eggs danced out of her shaking hand and splatted on the floor. Only three remained, so she carefully gathered them into her apron and took them to the bowl by the dry sink.

She could feel Clive's hot breath on her neck even from this distance as she whisked the eggs. The skillet had warmed by now, as had the pot of bacon grease. She could take the pot and dash the hot grease into Clive's face if he'd take his attention off her. Why couldn't she think of a way to distract him? He'd probably guessed she was looking for a chance. His six-gun lay cocked beside his plate.

Why hadn't she grabbed Zak's pistol? *Lord, make my brain function.*

The eggs cooked to Clive's taste fast. Too fast. She plated them and set them before him. He'd have to turn his attention to the eggs. She still held the iron skillet in her hand.

Clive kept his eyes trained on her as he scooped the eggs, one spoonful at the time. "Put down that pan and get me the salt."

Reluctantly, she returned the pan to the stove.

The salt wasn't in its normal place. *Thank you, Lord. An excuse.* "I left it in my bedroom. Zak and I ate in there last night. I'll get it."

She dashed from the kitchen, fully expecting Clive to follow her. Fortunately, he did not.

This might be her only chance. She passed the bedroom and made for the front door in swift, soft steps. Praying the door wouldn't creak, she opened it and breathed freedom. She didn't stop to close it.

The loud slam of a chair hitting the floor put energy into her feet. She ran for all she was worth down the steps, across the yard—almost tripping over the dead man. If only she could reach the forest and some cover. She didn't have to look back to know Clive had his gun ready, and he was gaining on he.

Why didn't he just shoot her in the back like he did the lawman? Of course, he didn't want to leave any blood that would have to be cleaned up to avoid alerting the posse anything was amiss.

He'd dump her in her grave before shooting her.

Jeannie clawed the air, trying to reach for the relative safety of the trees. The rest of the posse had to be nearby. But Clive's labored breathing closed in, telling her it was futile. He wasn't a healthy man, but he had more speed than her, and he wasn't impeded by heavy skirts and petticoats. Why hadn't she thought to put on Pa's breeches this morning? Because she'd wanted to look good for Zak before he left.

Zak. She'd never see him again.

Lord, please help me.

Clive grabbed a fistful of skirt, and her body jack-knifed. The stench of those horrible cigars he smoked hit her, then a sinew-corded arm circled her middle. The cold metal of the pistol barrel pressed into her temple. It was over. She'd never see Pa or Rose again.

But Ma and Jesus waited. Jeannie scrunched her eyes closed, preparing for the bullet's impact. Clive's rasping to catch his breath would be the last sound she'd hear.

Instead of a bullet, the thunder of horses' hooves penetrated her brain. She dared a peep. Several armed men rode into view. Clive saw them too. He jerked her around, never moving his gun.

He must know he couldn't get away now. That would hardly matter to him—he'd kill her anyway. He had nothing to lose.

Before she could even take it all in, a tan-sleeved arm appeared from behind and slammed down on Clive's gun. At the same time a force sent her flying out of Clive's clutches and into the bushes.

Jeannie crawled behind the nearest tree, a young Aspen whose trunk afforded little protection from flying bullets. Hugging the tree, she slanted her gaze toward the deadly scene, seeking out the face of her rescuer.

She held her breath as she recognized Zak. He had his pistol trained on the old man, but Clive still clutched his weapon.

Why didn't Zak fire?

Chapter 11

Why didn't Clive fire? The crazy man whirled around, putting his back to Zak. That was why. He knew Zak wouldn't shoot him in the back. But didn't he see the sheriff coming after him with raised rifle?

"It's over, Clive Stubbs," the sheriff shouted. Two of the men had gone to the fallen man. Two others anchored the sheriff who yelled again. "We caught Horace alive. Throw down your gun."

As if he didn't hear a word, Clive walked straight toward the sheriff.

He was trying to commit suicide.

"Stop there, Clive, I'm warning—"

Clive fired, though he must have known he was too far away from the sheriff to hit him with a pistol's bullet.

The rifle boomed, echoing through the forest. Clive swayed like a severed tree that didn't know which way to fall. He toppled on his back, the hole in his chest blooming red.

Zak squatted down beside him, but Clive didn't have enough life left in him to even twitch.

Jeannie.

She was at his side when he stood, and he pulled her into a hug. "I had my sights on him, Jeannie, and I couldn't fire."

"I'm glad. And strangely, Clive had a chance to shoot me, and yet he didn't. Maybe he had a change of heart at the last minute."

Zak tugged her closer. If it comforted Jeannie to think that, so be it, but he didn't believe much in death-bed conversions.

Sheriff Simmons strode up. "Tom and Jake are taking Sam back to town to see Doc. They'll send the undertaker back for Clive."

"Sam's not dead?"

"Nah, you can't kill that old coot. He knew to play dead until we got here. He's lost a lot of blood, though." The sheriff lifted his hat as his gaze scanned the horizon. "Better get back to where I lashed Horace to that tree. "I'll give you a few minutes with the lady."

Zak and Jeannie walked arm in arm to the porch steps.

"I'll testify on your behalf, Zak." Love and concern showed in Jeannie's eyes. "I'll tell them how you kept me safe. How you shielded me from those two brutes."

He searched her features. What was she talking about? Then it dawned on him she didn't know what was going on. He smiled and squeezed her hands. "You don't have to testify for me, Jeannie."

"But I will, no one will believe you're an outlaw when I finish. I feel responsible for you getting caught by hiding that message in Rose's cloak."

He slipped a hand in his pants pocket and drew out a slip of paper. "Is this what you're talking about?"

She took the paper, her fawn-colored eyes widening. "I don't understand."

"It was a clever move, Jeannie, and would've worked—except I'm a detective."

"A detective?" Her mouth fell open as her brows crooked in astonishment.

He had to smile at her reaction. "That's right, and I couldn't let those friends of yours get involved. If the local law had captured Clive and Horace, the Jackal would've sent in an army to shoot up that little town, and a lot of innocent people could've been killed."

"You were working against the gang? But he..." She pointed to Clive. "He was your pa."

"The fact is, I've been working with the law. Actually, I'm a Pinkerton agent. But Clive was my step-pa. Fact is, he's the reason I became an agent."

"I don't understand."

"I know you don't, honey." He slipped an arm around her, and they sat on the porch steps. "I ran away after Clive killed my ma, and the law ruled it an accident. Later, I heard Clive had joined one of the Jackal's gangs. One day I was walking by a Pinkerton office and saw my chance for revenge. Since I could watch Clive without raising any suspicion, I offered my services, and they trained me to be an agent. I came back and convinced Clive I wanted to join up. The plan was for him to lead me to the Jackal. I didn't know at the time I had to prove myself by killing someone. It was then I decided to kill him after we found out the identity of the Jackal."

"That's why you told Clive you'd kill me?"

The words still stung even though the danger had passed. He shifted and took one of her small hands in both his. "It was all I could think of to keep him from killing you. I want to tell you all of it, Jeannie, but you must promise not to utter this to another soul, not even your pa."

"I promise."

"The original plan was to follow Clive and Horace to the Jackal's hideout. I'd act as their scout and assure them the law was off our trail, when in fact, I'd alert the lawmen of our movements."

He smiled, caressing her knuckles with his thumbs. "You threw a wrench in those plans. I knew Clive wouldn't leave you alive, so I convinced him if I married you and took you along with us, I'd shoot you in front of the Jackal. Killing my own wife to protect the gang would be an act so diabolical even the Jackal would be convinced I was bad enough to join them. What I really intended to do was slip away with you when we located the Jackal's hideout. With you safely away, the posse would descend on the hideout."

"But you still don't know where the Jackal is, and Clive is dead."

"But Horace knows where to go, and he'll cooperate if he wants to save his sorry hide. I'll go in with Horace, and the posse will follow."

She grabbed his arm. "Don't go, Zak. It's too dangerous. I'm sure this Jackal, whoever he is, is well fortified."

"We have a new plan, Jeannie. I'm not going to discuss it, but it depends on me more than ever now. I have to go."

"But Zak—"

He brushed her hair back. "Does the concern I see in your eyes mean you've come to care for me a little?"

She blushed and looked away. "I know we haven't known each other but a few days, but what went on during those days seems like a lifetime. I'd be lying if I said I don't care. Truth is, I don't want you to risk your life. It's like God has brought you to me, and now He's snatching you away."

"I don't believe that for one moment, and you don't either. You have a lot more faith than that, Jeannie. I'm going to do everything in my power to come back to you. I promise you that. You have to pray for the rest."

The sound of men talking grew closer. "You ready, Zak?" The sheriff said, going to his horse. Another lawman came along with Horace in cuffs.

He rose and she jumped to her feet along with him. He cupped her chin and drew in for a farewell kiss. One to remember and cherish—like a soldier going into battle cherishes that last kiss.

She held on to him. "When will you be back?"

The men, saddled and impatient, waited for him. He stepped backwards. Still holding her hand, he brushed her fingertips with his lips. "I'll be away not a second longer than I have to."

Chapter 12

Nothing but hard work and faith sustained Jeannie through the next days and weeks.

Pa returned with a fine bull, a half dozen heifers, and a determination to build up the herd. Jeannie thanked the Lord for that. Engrossed in work, he was too busy to notice her anxiety. She wished it were possible to confide in Pa or Rose, but Zak and the lawmen who rode with him were on a secret mission. She feared even a hint of her involvement would endanger them.

Zak pervaded her thoughts as she harvested her vegetables, carried out the monotonous daily chores, and her dreams at night. Prayers drifted from her heart with every motion and every moment of rest. Despite that, time chipped away at her faith.

She never wavered from the belief, that had Zak not been detained—if he still lived—he'd come back to her. Each passing day strengthened the possibility she'd never see him again, and that niggling doubt clung to her like nettles to her skirt tail as she searched for huckleberries.

Zak's words replayed through her mind, both comforting and tormenting her. His touch still burned. His brief kisses haunted her. Each night, lying in bed, her gaze lingered on the spot where his pallet had been. Summoning all the hope she could, she prayed until sleep claimed her.

Rose's baby came, giving Jeannie a respite from her agony. Little Sara Marie, a healthy baby girl, provided an excuse to visit her friend more often. Twice a week, she got up early to make the long trek to the James ranch, taking peas and beans in a gunny sack slung over Pat's shoulders.

Pauline and Jeannie canned the vegetables, while Rose cared for her new infant. Pauline insisted on doing most of the work so Jeannie could play with the baby.

Gratefully, Jeannie took advantage to sit with Rose and watch the antics of the newborn. "Look Rose, she smiled at me." She held the squirming bundle on her knees, urging the baby's coos.

Rose peeked over Jeannie's shoulder. "She recognizes her Aunt Jeannie."

Instead of elating Jeannie, as the words should have, a cloud of melancholy descended. Would she have to settle for being an aunt to her friend's children? Never know the joy of becoming a mother. Never bask in the love of her child's father?

Sara's perfect, tiny digits grabbed Jeannie's finger, bringing a lump to her throat. Her chest tightened and the backs of her eyes burned. She forced a smile as she handed the baby to Rose. "I really must be going. It'll be dark before I get home."

The screen door slammed, cutting off anything Rose might say. Willie strode into the parlor with Billy dogging his steps. "Evening Jeannie." He nodded in her direction and went straight to Rose, bending to kiss his daughter's downy head. "How's my little princess doing?"

Rose laughed. "He used to kiss me first thing."

"Can I hold the baby, Ma?" Billy asked.

Pauline stuck her head around the corner from the kitchen. "Billy, if you'll come help me put the lids on my jars, I'll give you a licorice stick." Billy forgot his sister and dashed to the kitchen.

"Bring the buckboard next time, Jeannie, so you can get your share of the canning." Pauline wiped her brow with the corner of her apron. Canning was a hot job, and Jeannie felt guilty leaving most of the work to Pauline.

"I will," she said on her way to the door. She'd do more than her share next time. Somehow, she had to pull herself together and realize the world didn't revolve around her problems. But that wouldn't happen until she knew what happened to Zak.

The screen door's hinges squealed as she pushed against it, then she turned. "Willie, is there a Pinkerton Agency office closer than Chicago? Is there one in Medicine Bow?"

Rose and Willie exchanged a glance. "I really don't know. Why'd you be wanting to know something like that?" Willie laughed.

"One of those dime novels Pa brought back was about a Pinkerton Agent." She smiled, trying to show how little she cared. "I was just curious." That wasn't a total lie. Pa had brought her such a book, and she'd read it half a dozen times, since it gave her a glimpse into Zak's work.

"Good-night then. Pa and I will be by Sunday." But Rose and Willie weren't listening. They were engrossed, as only new parents could be, over little Sara.

The little tableau of baby and doting parents

struck Jeannie with such sadness, tears welled and spilled over. She closed the door behind her and raced to untether Pat. Once in the saddle, she urged him into a gallop.

The tears flowed unabated, but she didn't care. No amount of tears would help. There came a time when not knowing was worse than knowing the worse. She'd reached that point.

Somehow, she'd find the address of the nearest Pinkerton office and write for information. Even if the secret operation was still active, she'd ask about Zak in a round-about way.

A new thought darted to the surface. She still had Zak's pistol. That was the perfect way to explain her interest. She'd ask for his current address, so she could return the gun to him. If he were dead, they'd tell her that. If he lived but had forgotten about her, she'd know that too.

The wind had dried her tear-soaked face by the time the weathered ranch house came into view. As she rounded the trail, she noticed an unfamiliar horse tied to the hitching post. Pa had company, and judging by the time of day, the guest intended to stay for supper.

"Giddy-up, ole son. Looks like I'll have to lay another plate, which means I've got to get cooking." She cantered into the yard, keeping a steady stare on the strange horse that appeared less strange the closer she got.

Something familiar about the long-legged buckskin stallion sent goose-bumps up her arms. Pat reared to a halt as she pulled on the reins and slid out of the saddle before coming to a full stop.

Her heart flew into her throat.

Zak's horse.

In her haste, she forgot to lift her skirts and stumbled up the porch steps. After righting herself, she smoothed the folds of her old blue checkered dress. She must look a mess, but no worse than he'd seen her before. Her hands patted the wild tendrils of hair back in place as best she could. Already she could hear men's voices coming from within.

Just because the horse belonged to Zak, that didn't mean he was inside. One of his friends might have come to tell them the sad outcome.

She gripped the door handle. *Please God, let it be him.*

The pleasant fragrance of Pa's pipe tobacco hit her when she stepped inside. He stood at the mantle, gesturing to his guest with the pipe. Seated on the sofa, the other man had his back to Jeannie.

The door thudded behind her, and Pa looked up, his moustache widening with his smile. "Here she is now."

She held her breath, frozen to the floor. Since the guest's left shoulder and arm were encased in bandages, he got to his feet with some difficulty before turning to face her.

If she didn't remember Zak so well, she wouldn't have recognized him. His lean frame still filled out his chambray shirt and denims well, though he'd lost weight. But the change in his appearance astonished her. He'd shortened that wavy, dark hair she'd loved so much, and his clean-shaven cheeks revealed the planes of his handsome face, the smile lines punctuating his mouth. Instead of appearing younger, as was the case with many beardless men, Zak looked older—rakish even—due to the black patch covering his left eye.

His one good eye locked with hers for a long moment as she struggled to catch her breath. The look of two people reunited with their soul mate. "Jeannie." He held out his free arm.

Her wobbly legs gained strength, and she flew to his side. Ignoring Pa and all sense of propriety, she flung her arms around his waist. "You're alive."

He chuckled as if to release the tension. "I am, though it was touch and go for awhile, but if I'd lost the use of all my limbs and both my eyes, I'd have returned to you, even if I'd had to crawl all the way."

Pa came around on Zak's side and, laying a

hand on his injured shoulder, leaned in. "I guess I have my answer." He winked at Jeannie. "I'll be out on the porch."

Jeannie waited until Pa crossed the room and disappeared through the door, then she tugged Zak back to the sofa. "What happened?"

"There was a shoot-out. I took four bullets, but was blessed with three miracles." He pointed to his patched eye. "Doctors said this one came within a hair of my brain. That was the first miracle." He patted his bandaged chest. "This one missed my heart, but collapsed a lung and set up an infection that like to have taken me—the second miracle."

He paused, looking at her like he'd forgotten what he was talking about. "What was the third miracle?" she asked.

"You, Jeannie. I knew your prayers were winging their way to me."

She nodded. "They were—constantly."

"God heard you, Jeannie. While I was lying there for days, hovering between life and death, the Lord penetrated my stubborn will, and I came back home...like the prodigal." He reached out and tucked a wayward curl behind her ear, sending a delicious tingle down her spine.

"But they did get the Jackal?"

"He was killed along with a number of his gang and—I'm not going any further than that. Suffice it to say, putting down the Jackal's gang will save a good number of innocent people."

He was trying to spare her the gory details, so she wouldn't press him. "What did Pa mean, he had his answer?"

"Ah, that's what I want to talk about. Your pa and I had a long discussion. I asked him for permission to court you, but I told him with or without permission, I was going to ask you to marry me, broken as I am, because I love you with all my heart."

He coughed and silence fell between them. He'd just confirmed what she'd felt. Dreamed about. She'd heard the emotion and tension in his voice. Now that the moment had come, he was having trouble forming the question. Amazingly, they were so attuned, she could read his mind.

"What did Pa say?"

Zak's shoulders relaxed. "Your pa's a good man. He not only gave his permission but offered me a proposition. If you'd have me, he offered me a partnership in the ranch. I have some money saved, and we could increase the herds. It's something I've always wanted to do—ranching, and of course, I'm not physically able to carry on as a detective."

He took her hand and turned it palm up. "So it comes down to this. My future happiness lies in your small hand. May I have it in marriage?"

She ignored the tears spilling down her cheeks. "Of course. I love you more than anyone except the Lord Himself." She could say so much more but why waste the moment on words.

With eyes closed, she tipped her head to taste his kiss. Tender. Fervent. Wistful. Promising to bind them with love for a lifetime.

Author's Note

Thank you, dear reader, for reading *Cloaked in Love*. If you enjoyed this book, please leave a review at Amazon.com and Goodreads. I write only for the Lord's glory and the reader's pleasure, so I would much appreciate your opinion.

Other Books by this Author

Annex Mail Order Brides Series:

Book 1 - *Adela's Prairie Suitor*

Book 2 - *Ramee's Fugitive Cowboy*

Book 3 - *Prudie's Mountain Man*

Intrigue under Western Skies Series:

Book 1 – *Pursued*

Also:

The Perfect Gift, a Christmas Novella

About the Author

Elaine Manders writes wholesome, Christian romance about the strong, capable women of history and the men who love them. She prefers stories that twist and turn and surprise, told by characters who aren't afraid to show their love for God and each other. She lives in Central Georgia with her husband, Robert, and an energetic bichon-poodle mix.

You may contact the author at:

Facebook:

https://www.facebook.com/elaine.manders.35

Twitter: https://twitter.com/ehmanders

Blog: https://elainemanders.wordpress.com

Email: elainehmanders@gmail.com

Made in the USA
Charleston, SC
02 June 2016